Tenerite Noir

The first Danny Mclinden Adventure
Book 1: The Black Cane

By Mick Lee

First Published in 2021 by Mick Lee

Written by Mick Lee

Editing by Anne Grange Writing

Copyright © Mick Lee 2021

Cover photograph © Steve Belcher

Many thanks to Steve Belcher for the cover photo of Golf del Sur, Tenerife

All rights reserved. No part of this publication may be reproduced, stored in a retrieval system, or transmitted in any form or by any means, electronic, mechanical, photocopying, recording, or otherwise, without the prior permission of the author.

This book or any portion thereof may not be reproduced or used in any manner whatsoever without the express written permission of the publisher except for the use of brief quotations in a book review or scholarly journal.

ISBN:

9798705239351

Part One

Chapter One

The information that I was skint came in a phone call on my mobile from a nice Mr Patel from Lloyds Bank. Apparently the £500,000 compensation from my accident had been removed from the account and although my disability pension had been paid, this had mostly all gone on standing orders and direct debits.

I tried to ring my wife, Laura, but her mobile didn't connect. I left it a day, then tried again a couple of times before I rang an ex-colleague and asked him to pop round to my home to find out what was going on. An hour later, he was on the phone.

'She's gone, Danny.'

'What do you mean, gone?'

'There are people living there. They bought the house from Laura – knockdown price apparently.'

'I don't understand.' I told him about the call from Mr Patel.

'Danny, mate, you've been screwed over.'

I should explain my circumstances. My name is Danny Mclinden. I was a cop, and I was having these conversations from a nice apartment in Golf del Sur, Tenerife. I had been dispatched there by my wife of seven years in the belief that she would shortly follow me.

Whilst I am not wheelchair-bound any more, I am reliant on crutches, my speech is impeded, and my reactions are dulled due to an injury I sustained falling fifty feet through a roof. I was chasing two smack heads who had carried out a violent home invasion on two married pensioners, causing them serious injuries.

My knees are shot, and I've had them both replaced. The worst thing is the tinnitus – the permanent ringing in my ears. They had tried me on various drugs, but they didn't work; it was torture.

One day a physio suggested I got some music on my iPhone and some ear buds so that maybe the music could mask the noise. Over time, it worked. I think that by focusing on the music, I retrained my brain to adjust and I was able to cope. So now, every waking moment, I had a soundtrack playing in the background.

I used to be a cop, a good one, next in line for a promotion after three years in uniform and five years in CID. The day after my accident, I was supposed to be seeing the CID Chief Inspector who was going to induct me into my new role as Detective Sergeant.

Instead, I was on life support attached to a ventilator; induced coma, the full menu; my life effectively over before I reached forty.

Either side of me in the small ward were smackheads one and two. They too had fallen through the roof and were in a worse state than me. One visitor compared the scene to Golgotha, with me as Jesus and the smackheads as the thieves. The difference was Jesus forgave the thieves. Their condition was a small compensation I wasn't aware of at the time but from which I have derived a certain morbid satisfaction ever since.

***

The apartment was really nice, if small, with one bedroom. You entered on a level with the street, but at the front facing the sea, the level fell away and you were about four floors above the sea and central to the coastal footpath that stretched miles to the north and south, joining the windswept hippyish El Medano to the hedonistic delights of Playa de las Americas. A lift conveyed you to the path and the cafes and restaurants that lined the route leading to the Marina.

Laura had been thoughtful in her treachery: the fridge and freezer were stocked with food and an ample supply of Vina Sol and Corona beer, enough to keep me for two weeks. I had been pushed onto the plane, leaving the UK in a wheelchair and had been met at the other end with a Spanish bloke with another wheelchair.

A specialized taxi got me to the apartment, and the driver got me through the door, made sure I was safe, and left.

Mild panic set in as soon as I was alone. Laura had often left me alone in the house during my recovery, but I always knew that she'd be back. But I knew no one here. I could barely talk, or walk.

Actually, the panic helped. I got my crutches and stood up. For the first time in many months, my brain started to work. I made a sandwich, opened a bottle of Corona, and had a quick stumble round the apartment.

Unaware of the situation at home in the UK, I opened my suitcase and carefully hung the spare trousers and the three shirts I'd packed in the wardrobe and put my socks and pants in the drawer. Razor, toothbrush, and toiletries were placed in the requisite positions in the bathroom.

All my unpacking was done in a way to ensure that when Laura got there, she would find plenty of room for her stuff. In all, it took me about an hour to do chores I would normally have done in a quarter of the time.

I texted Laura to say that I had arrived, and all was OK. I got no response but thought that it was due to the distance between us or the various modes of signal transmission sorting themselves out.

I went to bed and the panic subsided. I was alone, but I could cope till she got here. It had been a long day. I pictured Laura waving me off as I went through the check in.

'See you in a couple of days.'

Those were her last words to me. She turned her back to leave as the guy pushed me through to the plane. I've haven't seen or heard of her since.

The next day, following the call from Mr Patel, and the info from my ex-colleague, was as they say, life changing. The strange thing was, as my ability to rationalise seemed to improve, that I wasn't that surprised.

I made breakfast and sat on the balcony. I had 500 euros in cash in my wallet, along with worthless credit and debit cards. I had no idea what to do. There was no one to phone – my parents were dead, and I was their only kid. They'd left me enough to buy my home outright and I shared the ownership with Laura. I never got to the bottom of how she had managed to sell it. Our house was worth about £350,000. She had therefore taken me for about £850,000.

I decided to give it a day or two, then maybe get a return ticket, go home, and throw myself on the mercy of the decreasingly generous British social security system. The future looked bleak.

My music was coming in through the ear buds: Martha Reeves and the Vandellas' 'Quicksand' playing in the background. *Yes, Martha, that's exactly how it feels. Sinking.*

That evening, I made a meal and took out a bottle of Vina Sol. I sat on the balcony watching the world go by and as I downed the bottle, I felt in need of company.

I had spotted a bar on the way into the apartment. Oddly named The Tame Duck, it was straight across the road. I showered and shaved. Feeling faintly human, I took my crutches and hobbled along the passageway that led to the street and the delights of the bar that was, unbeknown to me, going to play an important part in my future.

It was a big place, run down, capable of holding about a hundred. Tables and chairs were gathered around the bar to accommodate about thirty. A basic bar menu for food, booze, and a well-stocked, male-oriented bar with a number of tall stools fronting it.

I clambered onto one of the bar stools, parked the crutches, and ordered a Johnnie Walker Black with ice. Tenerife measures are generous and after a couple, topping up the already consumed Vina Sol, I was feeling the effect.

The barman was keeping his eye on me.

'You alright, buddy?' Irish accent, probably Dublin. He extended his hand for me to shake. 'The name's Shaun.'

'I've been better, Shaun,' I muttered.

In the time-honoured fashion of good barmen, he'd identified a man in need. As we approached closing time and the punters started to disperse, he asked me what the problem was, and I opened up to him, telling him everything.

He continued to top up my glass, and by the time he had collected the glasses and wiped the bar top, he was familiar with my accident, the desertion and pillage of my wife and the fact that I was completely and utterly 'fooked', to use the Irishism he'd used.

Shaun offered to get me home, He locked up the bar as I stood wobbling on the crutches outside the bar and he walked me across the street, carefully ensuring I didn't fall.

Shaun had got me back to the apartment, but I was drunk as a skunk. The alcohol, doing the job it was intended to, was numbing the depression and the fear. He took the crutches from me and dropped me, fully clothed, on the bed.

'Now, when you wake up, come down to the bar and I'll treat you to a nice Irish breakfast. Sleep well, Danny. It's always darkest before the dawn.'

Chapter Two

Buddy Guy was singing 'A Few Good Years' through my EarPods. *I'd had a few, Buddy*, but the future, even through the Johnnie Walker-induced haze, was looking grim.

The knock was quiet but persistent. I got to my feet.

'Hang on a minute,' I managed to mumble.

The sun was streaming in through the windows from the east. I grabbed the crutches and made my way to the door. Opening it, I was confronted by a large man in his mid-forties. He was wearing a Boston Bruins baseball cap, a Hawaiian shirt, cargo shorts and a big smile.

'Hi, I guess you are Danny. I'm a friend of Shaun's, from the bar. Mind if I come in?' Yank. Southern drawl.

Other than Shaun the night before, I had not really spoken to anyone for more than a few sentences for over two years, so the thought of a long conversation worried me a little. I beckoned him inside and he sat in the shade as the sunlight streamed in through the open patio window leading to the balcony.

My head was banging following last night's wine and whisky and my ear pods had fallen out. The tinnitus was in full flow and I excused myself.

After a pee and throwing some water over my head, I reinserted the pods and heard the reassuring voice of Barry Gibb singing 'In the Now'. *OK Barry, thanks for that. Focus.*

I hobbled over and sat opposite my visitor, who introduced himself, and fixed me with that look of false sincerity the Americans are good at.

'I'm Grant. Shaun told me about you. I'm really sorry about your problems but I may be able to help. I understand you're alone in the world, what with you wife leaving you with all your treasure and such.'

I nodded. The strange thing was that, despite the booze haze, the other haze caused by the bang to my head seemed to be clearing. I guessed it was due to the shock of finding out about Laura's treachery. Maybe it was the high-altitude plane journey, or maybe just the booze, but I was actually able to concentrate more.

'I'm levelling with you because clearly you aren't a drug enforcement or MI5 guy,' he said, still smiling broadly. 'I know you're an ex-cop, but I guess you were more of a what the Metropolitan Police used to call a 'woodentop', so I'm not scared…'

'And what would you have to be afraid of?' I said, trying to keep the suspicion out of my voice.

'Danny, I'm a smuggler. I move drugs from South America, diamonds from West Africa and guns and ammo anywhere where people have the money to buy them.' Still the smile.

My mouth falling open at this point must have added to the wonky impression already given by my inability to string a sentence together and my ungainly method of moving around.

'So if you tell anyone about this conversation, they won't believe you. You'll be seen as a brain damaged cripple who's received bad news and is clearly deluded – and by the way, if that doesn't work, I will kill you.'

He maintained the smile; indeed, it may have broadened a bit as he said this. I tried to smile back until he reached into his waistband and produced a small pistol.

The 'woodentop' crack was a bit unfair, but, in light of the gun, who was I to argue?

'What do you want me to do?' My concentration level was improving by the millisecond.

'In my car there are a number of kit bags. They contain five million Euros – mostly in 500 Euro notes. I want to leave them with you in this apartment. It's nearly midday. In twelve hours – about midnight tonight, a yacht will sail into the Marina. It's called the Monte. Once it enters the harbour, the guys on board will phone you. You phone a taxi – there are still some around at midnight – load the bags into it. The driver will help you.

Meet the yacht as it moors, just let the guys on board take the bags.'

I just sat and listened, taking all this in. From two years of virtually complete inaction, within the last few hours, I had become homeless, penniless and my wife had deserted me, and now, to top it all, I was sat opposite a modern-day version of Captain Kidd, who was making me the smugglers' version of an offer I couldn't refuse.

'What's in it for me, Grant?'

'Stay cool for twelve hours and you take twelve grand out of a bag. If the boat is late, you take a grand for every hour.'

I sat back in the chair, alarmed at the prospect of becoming a serious criminal, weighing my options. Who would I tell? Who would believe me? Who could understand what I was saying? The Guardia Civil have a great many speakers of English, but how they would cope with someone in my condition, god only knows.

On the other hand, I was skint and alone in the world. I had been a straight copper, but then again, no one had ever offered me enough to tempt me.

Why not do it? If I got caught, I would get locked up. At least I'd get fed – I like Spanish food, maybe they had Paella. While I was banged up, I was sure committees and action groups would form in the UK, demanding my release. I could see the headlines: *'Brain Damaged Police Hero in Spanish Hell-Hole*

Jail.' The tabloids would love it. Philip Schofield and that blonde bird would be all over it, as would those boring people who man the BBC news settee.

I could become a personality. On the other hand, if I refused, I'd return to the UK to live under a cardboard box. Also, the chances of Captain Kidd, still sitting nonchalantly opposite me, leaving this room with me alive were less than even.

'Yeah, fuck it, why not,' I mumbled. 'Nothing to lose – twelve grand would be very handy.'

'You stay here. Give me your phone number and delete your contacts so you won't be tempted to call anyone. Just in case you decide to do something crazy, I want you to know that you can't get to the airport, let alone get on a plane without me knowing.' He handed me a card for a taxi company. 'Use this later,' he added. 'And keep the phone charged. If I want you, I'll call. Twelve hours – then your life changes for the better.'

In my headphones, Yvonne Ellman was singing 'If I Can't Have You, I Don't Want Anybody'. *Nice song, Yvonne – totally irrelevant to the current situation.*

Grant stood up. 'I'll be back in a few minutes.'

I waited, pondering on the wisdom of this plan, wondering if my head injury had made me a little mad. The good thing was that all this activity had cleared my head, and it appeared to be staying that way.

Grant returned with two big bags on his back and carrying two more, one other in each hand. *So that's what five million Euros looks like.*

'Most of the cash is in five hundred notes. Don't try to cash one in a bar or somewhere crazy – there's some small change in there that is near enough your twelve grand – take that.'

I sat looking up at him. He smiled, walked into the bedroom, and pushed the bags under the bed.

'Don't forget. Stay cool for twelve hours, and you take twelve grand. Glen Frey was singing 'Smugglers Blues'. *Nice song – totally relevant to the current situation.*

Chapter Three

Once Grant left the apartment, I made breakfast. One side of my brain was telling me: *panic, call the cops, get out of this.* The other was saying: *what the hell, you've nothing to lose, if you're caught, act daft, you'll get away with it.*

I took the coffee and the toast and sat out on the balcony, where I had a perfect view of the Marina, its entrance, and anything approaching it from miles away.

Time passed. I watched people do what they do on holiday: walking about – seldom alone, there were couples, families, and friends. I wondered about Laura, and about the friends I used to have before I submerged myself in Police work – and the incident that nearly killed me. I wasn't a good husband. I lived for work. I think Laura tried to stay strong for me after my accident, but, embittered as I was about the circumstances, in a way, I understood.

She had been solicitous at first, becoming a devoted Florence Nightingale when visitors, invariably other cops, came to visit. As these visits became less frequent, she drank wine and ate crisps, slowly piling on weight and coming to detest herself and the drooling numpty in the wheelchair.

After about a year, she started to go to a nearby gym. The sessions got longer, and she was regularly out for most of the morning. By this time, I could get to the lavatory, and wash myself. Later, the medics arranged for me to have handrails fitted in the shower and I had actually showered myself independently a few times before I got packed off to the apartment.

Laura's gym sessions had the desired effect and soon she was losing weight and looking good. She started going out on weekend nights. The physio exercises she was supposed to be putting me through became less and less frequent as her social activity increased. In my stupor, I never realised what was happening. She had met another bloke, and together they set about ruining my financial health as much as my fall had affected my physical and mental health.

Watching the promenaders below my balcony made me sad, but maybe the bang on the head had adjusted my moral compass. I had been screwed, physically and emotionally. No one cared, so why should I? It was time to start a comeback.

I found a YouTube site with exercises for people in rehabilitation and did some basic exercises. On the small bookshelf in the apartment were some adventure stories. I read a book for the first time in two years. I was pleased at the way my head had unfogged. Jamie Cullum was singing 'All at Sea'. *Thanks, Jamie, I'm not as bad as I was.*

The night came quickly, as it does in the Canaries. One minute it was warm and sunny, the next, the warmth started to dissipate, and the light went. The boats and walkways in the

Marina started to light up, and the people started to fill the restaurants and bars, cajoled into entering them by the numerous greeters and touts employed to encourage wavering customers into their particular establishments.

I showered, with the usual difficulty, shaved and changed. I hung my two changes of clothes in the wardrobe and placed the soiled stuff in the small washing machine. Time to get organized. After all, I was now a criminal, and I may as well be a well-organised one.

Dinner was a chicken breast, which I stuffed with mushrooms and herbs, and served with a little pasta and a green salad. I looked at the bottles of Vina Sol. Laura had at least made sure I had supplies. In view of the need to stay sharp, I declined its temptation and opened a bottle of Corona, ice cold.

I took dinner on the balcony. I was very happy to note that my changed condition and the apparent relief within my head had led me to stop drooling. I could eat and drink almost normally.

I decided to take a look at the money. I dragged one of the bags out and opened it. It was full to the brim with 500 Euro notes. I didn't bother counting till I got to the bag containing the lower denominations. That, I got out and counted. It was in fifties mostly, with some twenties, even a few tens.

I counted out my twelve grand. There was a heavy Spanish-style sideboard against one of the walls in the lounge with some space underneath, and I placed my cash there.

I then moved the remaining cash between the four bags until they were all roughly the same weight. Killing time, thinking, occasional doubts, weird elation. Excitement was doing something to my brain. I was feeling better than I had ever since they took me off the ventilator.

At ten o' clock, all was quiet on Golf del Sur. In my ears, Billy Holliday was singing 'I cover the Waterfront'. *So do I, Billy, so do I.*

I did two lots of the exercises and hobbled around the apartment, listening to the music. I read a little, avoiding the TV. Two years of the Jeremy Kyle show and the rest of the crap that infested British TV, whilst, for the most part, being wheelchair-bound and unable to operate a remote was enough for a lifetime. I resolved to avoid it as much as possible. That resolve was to be tested in the next few hours.

I had been off the opioids for a while now but they kept calling me back. I was still taking naproxen and paracetamol, but not all the time. I had a nap. I was feeling good. Nervous but good.

Midnight came. There were a decent pair of binoculars in the apartment. With them, I could see occasional lights from night fishermen out at sea. Apart from that, nothing was moving in the ocean. I had been observing the comings and goings at the Marina and nothing had moved since ten. Gary Moore sang 'Midnight Blues' in my ear. *Perfect timing, Gary.*

One in the morning. They owed me another grand. I got it out of the bag. Nothing was moving, apart from a Guardia Civil car patrolling around the marina. A cop got out for a smoke, eyeing a lovely catamaran. Barnes Courtenay was singing 'Glitter and Gold'. *Ting Ting, Barnes.*

Two o' clock. Nothing. Cop long gone. A cat patrolled the walkway, reacting nervously to a sound from a boat – probably someone snoring.

3am then 4am. Still nothing, they owed me 16k. I transferred it to my stash under the wardrobe.

At 4.10am, a light came from the south west, keeping close to the shore. It was dim but definitely there, heading for the turn into the marina. It had to be the Monte. I picked up the 24-hour taxi card that Grant gave me. Would there be a taxi available at this time in the morning? Of course there would be – flights left the island all the times.

My phone was fully charged, with a good signal. I waited for the call from the boat's crew. I guessed it would take the boat about fifteen minutes to get into the marina. I waited, fingers hovering over the phone's screen.

The boat blew up.

It went up like a brush fire, stem to stern. I dropped the phone and stared. I made it to the front door of the apartment as quickly as I was able, remembering the notice placed there by the owner about what to do in an emergency – who to call and for non-Spanish speakers, what to say.

I dialled the emergency number. The call taker was brilliant, although I was so shocked, my mumbling had returned, and I was virtually incapable of speech.

'Boat – fire – Marina – Golf del Sur,' was all I said.

Chapter Four

The sirens followed shortly afterwards. First the cops, then the fire brigade. They could do little more than stand on the marina wall and watch the boat burn. Eventually, a helicopter flew in, followed by a Guarda Civil launch. The fire appeared to be out, but black smoke still billowed from the hulk as the sun rose over the Red Rock to the east.

I sat on the balcony, looking out as the Police boat hooked a line onto the burned-out yacht and started to tow it into the safety of the Marina. I know now that these waters are very unpredictable and can change from millpond to very rough indeed in seconds. Obviously, the cops knew this and were keen to get it into safe waters.

My phone rang. I expected Grant – I got Sergeant Primero Oliva of the Tenerife Guardia Civil. He had traced my emergency call. He wanted to see me and was already on his way to my apartment.

His English wasn't good, and my Spanish was virtually non-existent. *Think*, I told myself. I opened the English to Spanish translator app on my iPhone and wrote:

I am an ex-Police officer from England. I am disabled due to injuries sustained on duty. If I appear unhelpful or disrespectful, it is because of my injuries. Good old Apple.

Sergeant Oliva arrived with a colleague. They were both in plain clothes, investigators. I stumbled around on my crutches, fumbled with the iPhone, and showed them the message.

In a genuine state of shock. I realised that the bags were stacked under the bed, visible to anyone. The sixteen thousand Euros I'd taken was out of sight. If they searched, I was in the shit.

The two policemen read the translation and stared at me. I mumbled, pointing out to sea. I said something even I couldn't understand. They humoured me. I pointed at my phone and the notice on the door with the emergency numbers. They understood and asked who was staying here with me.

I told them the truth. At least that bit would keep them sympathetic. They smiled and asked me why I was awake.

'I don't sleep too well – tinnitus,' I told them, typing the words into the translator as well as speaking English.

In my headphones, The Rolling Stones were playing 'It's All Over Now'. *No, it isn't, Mr Jagger – it's going rather well.*

They asked me if they could help me. I told them no, and they thanked me and left the apartment, both shaking my hand warmly.

While all this was happening, I was expecting the smuggler king Grant to appear at the door, or at least phone. There was nothing.

***

I spent the day watching the comings and goings in the Marina. a crowd had gathered – mostly tourists, but inquisitive locals too. The Fire Brigade had damped down the burning shell of the Monte and the cops were searching it, with a very motivated Belgian Malinois dog leading the hunt.

Night came. With still nothing from Grant, I decided to go back to the bar to see if Shaun had any information. I covered the bags with sheets, god knows why, and I checked my cash. I took a fifty. For the first time in my life, I had illegal cash in my pocket. *Accept it, you are a bandit*, I told myself.

The Tame Duck was fairly busy, with a couple serving behind the bar. I ordered a drink, sat down on the high stool, and parked the crutches.

'Is Shaun around?' I asked.

The new guy had a name badge that read Ronnie. The lady was Wendy.

'He had to go to La Gomera,' Ronnie said – the small island just over the straits from Tenerife.

'When's he back?'

'Should have been back this morning. We've been drafted in to cover him not turning up.'

We chatted. Ronnie was a Brummie, Wendy a Scouser. They were patient with my impaired speech – nice people, they run bars and work as entertainers; know the island like the back of their hands.

After I'd been there long enough to establish my enquiry about Shaun was not the reason for my visit, I returned to the apartment.

It was 10pm. Someone was sitting in the reception area. She was dark, tall, and buxom, with a serious expression on her face.

I entered on my crutches. Shambling towards my door, she approached me.

Taj Mahal was singing 'Waiting for the World to Change' in my earphones. *It might Taj. it just might.*

'Senor Danny Mclinden?'

'Yes Ma'am.'

'I am Ellen Perez. I am the welfare officer for the Guardia Civil. Sergeant Oliva tells me you are an English policeman recuperating from serious injury?'

'An ex-policeman, Ma'am.'

'Please call me Ellen.'

I'm getting rather good at this eliciting sympathy lark, I thought.

'Ellen.'

'Oliva called me to see if I can be if any assistance to you as a fellow Policia.'

She took my arm and we walked to the apartment. I fumbled with the keys and she took them from me. We entered, and she took the crutches as I stumbled towards a chair. She made coffee, and we sat down to talk.

'I think Sergeant Oliva thinks I am worse than I actually am – the shock of seeing the explosion really disturbed me. I'm damaged but not that damaged.'

She smiled. She was lovely, in that way Spanish women just past the first flush of youth are: well-fed, well-groomed, olive skin and oh that hair…

'Your wife?'

'Gone.'

'With your money?'

'It's not as bad as I first thought,' I replied, looking over her shoulder at the bags containing 4,984,000 euros.

The next day, I loyally sat in the apartment waiting for Grant to call. Nothing. I expected Shaun to turn up at the door. Nothing.

I broke my resolution regarding the telly and put on the local news. They were rattling along in fast Spanish when suddenly a picture of the marina came up with a burned-out boat secured to the harbour wall. The expression 'Dos Hombres' resonated quite a bit, as did 'Todos Muertos' and when the next pictures came up, clearly from Police records, I was glad I was seated.

Shaun Mcstefoin from Dublin and Grant Kidd from Charleston, South Carolina *(hey, he really was Captain Kidd)*, were named as the two victims. I had not expected this situation at all. My impression was that Grant, and indeed Shaun, would be ashore. I was confused and alarmed at the fact that they were actually both on the boat. What the hell was going on? Whose was this bloody money?

Songs from the Shows was playing in my ear: James Cagney singing 'Yankee Doodle'. I remembered that Charleston was the Confederate capital. As it was his hometown, Grant would not have been happy with that song. Then again, his parents had called him Grant, the name of the Yankee General that won the civil war. It makes you wonder, doesn't it? Or was this latest excitement making my brain damage manifest itself in a new way?

Chapter Five

Three weeks passed. I spent the days in the apartment, doing some exercises and reading. I got a little shopping in from the little supermarket just a few yards from the entrance to the apartment complex. I took time to cook, having downloaded some recipes via the iPhone.

I was tempted to drink in the daytime, but disciplined myself to leaving this till after 6pm, the time the sun sank over the proverbial and literal yardarms in the Marina that was becoming one of the central concerns of my life. My main worry was what was stored in the kit bags under my bed.

I contacted the agency who managed the apartment and extended the rental indefinitely. I was already feeling that whatever was going to happen, it wasn't going to be as quick as I thought, now that the two principals who knew about me had been incinerated.

I started to become a regular in the Tame Duck, where, after the initial shock of Shaun's sudden departure, things were continuing as normal under the management of Ronnie and Wendy. In fact, they were doing really well. The place had a capacity of about a hundred people but had become run down. They had cleaned the place up, were serving some half decent food and after about 9pm, got their backing tapes out and provided some good touristy entertainment.

The regulars were a mixed bunch, many of whom were retirees: couples, widows, and widowers. As the name suggests, Golf del Sur is a mecca for lovers of the fairways.

There were a number of British and Irish expats who had come to the island for the sun, sea, and its free and easy lifestyle. They included the bar and restaurant owners, the entertainers, water sports and adventure coaches, also builders, maintenance guys, plumbers and 'sparkies'.

This mix of residents, when added to the tourists, mostly Brits and Irish but increasingly from eastern Europe and the US, created a lively, friendly atmosphere, but with that underlying tension that an itinerant population brings.

One night, the bar stools were all full and I got my drink and hobbled over to a table. I was getting more mobile and the ability to sit in a normal bar room chair had been a challenge I wanted to take on. I was surprised at how well my knees bent.

The bar filled up and soon, three blokes came over and asked if the other chairs were free, I beckoned them to sit down, moving the crutches as I did so.

'You alright, pal?' A Manc, wearing a blue City shirt.

'Yes, thanks.'

'Had a knock, pal?' His mate, Manc Two, wearing the away shirt.

'Yeah, had a fall a couple of years ago – about fifty feet.'

'Fuckin' hell, lad, you're lucky to be around.' The third guy was a Yorkie; fat lad, Leeds United top.

'Banged me head mostly, makes me talk a bit funny, but I'm OK.'

We introduced ourselves. Manc One was Gary; Manc Two was Steve, and Matt the Yorkie. They were all builders, and as the evening wore on, I found they were ex-football hooligans and had been convicted for their misdemeanours.

After that revelation, I wasn't too surprised to find out that they were former members of the BNP, the National Front; indeed, anything likely to give them the opportunity to take part in serious street fighting. They got fined and even locked up a few times but eventually, looking at some serious jail time, they had unknowingly shared a barrister. The barrister had given them all the same advice: while they were awaiting trial, prior to conviction, they had all joined the Territorial Army.

This had been their only redeeming feature in the Judge's eyes, and it saved them from going to prison. The strange thing was that they loved the Territorials and their membership soon rivalled their football affiliations. They had met on an army training course and formed an informal brotherhood that would last as long as Man City stayed in the Premier and Leeds in the lower league.

If they ever drew each other in a cup match, carnage could easily have broken out. The truce had lasted several years so far, and the lads were doing well in their business, which was a combination of building services and diver training. The latter skill had been learned as members of the Territorials.

They adopted me and like a great many men who have revelled in violence, were kindness itself when dealing with someone who was incapacitated. Me being an ex-cop didn't bother them. When they heard of the way I had sustained my injuries, chasing smack heads who'd burgled and beaten up a couple of pensioners, my position, if not within the group, became that of an accepted outsider.

It became usual for me to sit with them. I didn't contribute much to the conversation and as I looked pretty vacant most of the time, they didn't seem to be concerned about me hearing anything confidential. One night, they mentioned Shaun. It seemed he was a popular guy, but with a few dodgy connections.

'His mate was that big yank – used to drink Southern Comfort and coke,' Steve said.

'I wonder why they were out on that boat – where had they been? Matt asked.

'Probably La Gomera, to see them Venezuelans,' Gary said.

'I don't like them Venezuelans – tricky twats,' Matt commented.

There were nods all round. Over the next few days, I found out there was a small community of Venezuelans on the neighbouring island of La Gomera. Eventually, I discovered that they were all involved in criminality. Mostly, they were involved in money laundering throughout the Canary Islands, but, if major drug routes were unavailable due to Police or Military activity, they acted as a storage facility for illegal drugs. The drugs were stashed there en-route from Central/South America by the Moroccan gangs who controlled their distribution throughout western Europe and kept there until it was considered safe to move them.

Gary and his friends had their suspicions that Grant and Shaun were somehow in cahoots with them. As the only person who saw the yacht before it exploded, I was sure its direction of travel was from the direction of La Gomera.

I realised the lads' capabilities one night when, out of the blue, a team of six jocks came in, Glasgow's finest: Celtic shirts, cussing anything English, out to cause mayhem.

Ronnie and Wendy had employed a couple of barmaids as trade had improved and one of them, pretty as a picture, went to serve the jocks. It was horrible. The young woman did her best, but nothing was good enough and glasses were smashed. Ronnie stepped in, got manhandled, and then Wendy went to assist and got backhanded.

No words were needed. The combined force of the Manchester City Guvnors and the Leeds United Service Crew sprang into action. It was as brutal as it was short. The jocks never got out of the corner. Groaning, and covered in blood and snot, they were dragged either unconscious or semi-conscious out of the bar.

One survivor got to his feet and picked up a wine bottle, attempting to cosh the Yorkie from behind. I stuck out my crutch, tripping him up, then whacked him on the head with it. He stayed down after that.

'Ey up, Danny,' said the Yorkie. 'Tha'rt a bit handy with them pegs.' He indicated my crutches. 'Thanks, pal.'

In my headphones, Alabama Three were singing 'Peace in the Valley'. *Not tonight, apparently.*

Chapter Six

Excellent Medical is, as the name suggests, a Health Centre in Golf del Sur. It is indeed excellent, providing a wide range of services from Psychiatry to Physiotherapy and from Ophthalmology to Liposuction.

I started a course of physiotherapy and got the doctors to give me the once over. I was improving, although the tinnitus was unrelenting.

The good thing was that my collection on my iPod exceeded 40,000 pieces of music and poems. I could talk to people quite easily as I got used to, accepted, and indeed enjoyed the fact that I had a musical soundtrack playing in the background 24/7. My knees were bad, and the physio said the best I could hope for was the permanent use of a walking stick.

So be it. If I had to have a stick, I'd have a good un. There was an African handicraft shop in the San Blas shopping Centre. I got a taxi there and had a look round. I found a heavy African blackwood cane. Decorated in West African symbols and designs, it would prove to be a stylish and useful aid. It might also come in handy if anyone came looking for their money.

That night, the Tame Duck was busy. Behind the bar, I thought Wendy seemed tearful. Ronnie was entertaining the punters, singing an old Lou Rawls song that suited his baritone. A few couples were dancing.

'Want another?' Wendy asked, as I finished my first drink.

'What's wrong?' I asked.

Wendy sighed.

'The bar's up for sale – we were just looking after it after Shaun died. The bank has traced the owner and they want to sell it off. We can't afford to make an offer.'

'That's such a shame – I know you love this place.'

I went home and slept on it. The next morning, I went for breakfast at the Tame Duck.

Ronnie greeted me and brought over the coffee. It was quiet and I asked him to sit down with me. We chatted and I after a while, I asked him if he fancied buying the place.

'I do,' he said, wistfully. 'But me and Wendy couldn't scrape that sort of cash together.'

'Do you fancy a sleeping partner?' I asked.

His eyes lit up for a second. Then he looked hopeless again.

'It's two hundred and fifty thousand Euros, Danny.'

That amount wouldn't even empty a quarter of one of the kit bags.

'You and Wendy can run it. I'll finance it. The only condition is that you never tell anyone where the cash came from – and never mention my name in connection with it.'

Ronnie opened his mouth in astonishment.

'Well, I've not got a problem with that, Danny.'

'There's only one problem – it has to be cash. This money isn't in my bank account.'

Ronnie thought for a moment. 'Leave it with me, Danny. I know a bloke.' After years on the Island, Ronnie knew lots of blokes.

'Sort it out, Ron, speak to the sellers – tell them they've got a better offer,' I told him.

***

Guillermo Cabrera was the chosen 'bloke' that Ronnie knew. According to his business card, he was a lawyer specializing in real estate, who helped to sell bolt holes to hard-working northern Europeans and retirement properties to those who wanted to spend their 'golden years' turning orange in the sun.

In fact, Guillermo was a Mr Fixit. He had made money during the Time Share scandals of the 90s and early 2000s. There wasn't a marginal or shady deal on the island that he didn't know about, or more likely, was involved in.

He walked a fine line regarding legality but was astute enough to never exactly cross it. He was fat, sweaty, moustachioed, loved his children; loved his wife, although, as I learned later, he was utterly terrified of her, for good reason.

Ronnie arranged for me to meet him the following lunchtime. Cabrera was standing at the bar in the Tame Duck, drinking coffee and talking to Ronnie, who introduced us. Ronnie had outlined the situation, and Cabrera had a broad, all-knowing smile that indicated there would be no problem.

There wasn't. I told him that I had the cash; that it was in the criminal's favourite denomination e.g., 500s and he nodded. We agreed that I would bring the cash later that afternoon.

The last thing I wanted anyone to know was that the cash was in my apartment, so, on leaving the bar, I hailed a cab and went for a trip into Los Christianos.

I asked the driver to wait while I hobbled into a hotel, where I killed five minutes, asked the receptionist for a carrier bag, filled it with paper hand towels and returned to the cab. Anyone following me would suspect I had stashed my cash in the hotel.

Returning to Golf del Sur, I went to the apartment, got rid of the paper towels and filled the bag with the 250,000 Euros I needed to pass to Cabrera. Then I waited.

I didn't think I had been followed but I kept the big stick close just in case. In the late afternoon, I took the cash into the bar and took my usual seat.

A few minutes later in, Cabrera came in, accompanied by Ronnie and Wendy. He took the cash and arranged to see us the next day. By lunchtime, the paperwork was completed, Ronnie and Wendy were the proud owners of the Tame Duck and I had a share in the business.

Cabrera took me aside. He had taken a commission out of the money and was clearly interested in the source of my wealth.

'Danny, I am not going to pry, but if I can be of service to you regarding making any monies you have a little more useable, please do not hesitate to ask.' He smiled and walked away. Tony Bennett was singing 'Rags to Riches.' *It's alright you going on, Bennett, I've got more money than Croesus and I haven't the faintest idea what to do with it.*

I took a chance. As the fat Spaniard walked away, I called out.

'Actually, Guillermo, there was something…'

Chapter Seven

Vatican City, home of the Pope and spiritual heart of the Roman Catholic religion, is also a leading centre for unlawful money laundering. Guillermo Cabrera had contacts there.

Some years previously, he had been to the Vatican to arrange the laundering of several million Euros being carried by criminals involved in the Time Share business. He had also 'washed' the proceeds of a few diamond trades and just a few deals regarding illegal arms. He avoided drugs. Too much competition, far too much *violenza*.

He entered the austere, somewhat forbidding entrance to the bank, where he was met by his host Signore Dallis, a man with whom he had dealt before. From Signore Dallis' point of view, this amount was chicken feed, a mere 4,500,000 Euros, but his commission would be generous, and he liked the fat Spaniard, an infrequent, but trouble-free client.

Cabrera didn't have tinnitus or a soundtrack playing in his ear, if he had, as he got on the plane to return to Tenerife, the tune should have been 'Arrivederci Roma'.

***

The money would be spread over several new accounts which would, in turn, feed into one master account in my name. The income derived would be shown to the taxman or anyone interested as my compensation payment, spectacularly well invested, the interest from which would be available to me monthly. Cabrera had charged me 250,000 Euros, the bank a further 300,000 Euros, leaving me with the interest on the best part of four million Euros, paid monthly, tax-free. Or well over eight thousand Euros per month. Kosher.

I was better paid than the Prime Minister. Also, the Duck was flying, meaning that the pub was doing really well. Ronnie and Wendy had done the place up a treat, with a smoking area at the rear with nice settees. They'd decorated right through and put in a small stage. Through their local show-biz contacts, they hired the best entertainers on the island. And they were bunging me a steady five thousand Euros a month.

Ronnie was doing what he was best at, and every night, he was immaculate in his evening suit. Think Humphrey Bogart in *Casablanca* introducing the acts; singing a little; sharing a little patter with the punters. Wendy was a great bar manager and businesswoman – the staff loved her. The place had become a goldmine.

Six months went by. I was now attending a local gym every day, as well as regular physiotherapy. My knees had not healed well after the replacements, largely because without Laura's supervision and help, it had been impossible to do the daily exercises necessary to ensure that my flexibility returned.

Frequent visits to the physio and the gym helped to remedy this.

I had also moved from the apartment to a nice two-bedroomed villa just a little down the coast towards Amarilla. It had a twenty-metre swimming pool and I used it daily. Although I was still in need of the walking stick, I had never been fitter. The villa wasn't cheap, but it came with a daily maid service and a pool guy.

I took most of my meals at the Duck, where Wendy had adopted, if not a maternal interest in me, certainly that of a big sister or a cool aunt. I ate well and healthily.

Cabrera called a couple of times a week and we had lunch, sometimes at the Duck, occasionally at one of the nearby cafes for a change. He was an interesting and entertaining companion, and I grew to like him a lot.

He had profited from our arrangement and was confident that all tracks were covered.

Then Mrs Cabrera got kidnapped.

Chapter Eight

I noticed the four missed calls on my iPhone as I left the gym. It was Guillermo.

'They have taken her, Danny – they have taken her!'

'What are you on about?'

'My wife, my Isabella, they have kidnapped her.'

'Who has?'

'Those Venezuelan bastardos – they know about the money – it was theirs.'

***

A week before this panicked conversation took place, Signore Dallis, he of the low-profile bank in Vatican City, had a visitor from La Gomera, a citizen of Venezuela. His name was Edwin Valero. He was representing an organization based in Central/South America, of which he was the European agent, his primary function being the maintenance of the partnership between his fellow countrymen and the Moroccan gang who were distributed throughout Europe and beyond.

Valero was seeking to deposit regular large amounts of cash with the bank. These could range from anywhere between $50 to $100 million in a range of denominations. This cash was the regular income derived from the Moroccan gang, who retailed the product once they had received it from the Venezuelans. Facilities were granted, and it was agreed that a private jet would arrive at a small airfield outside Rome once a month, containing the cash. Signore Dallis would make all the arrangements. The business concluded, Signore Dallis took his visitor to lunch.

Dallis was a careful man, as befits someone providing banking facilities for some of the world's most dangerous criminal enterprises. But he was unaware of the gaffe he made over lunch, when he mentioned that after many years of conducting business, he had never dealt with an enquiry from a potential client based in the Canaries before. Now, within the space of a few weeks, he'd had two, the other hailing from Tenerife.

He assured his visitor that the other client was trifling, a small deposit, more of a favour to an old friend than a profitable connection. Why, it was less than 10% of the amount they expected from La Gomera in any one month. He didn't confirm whether he actually had the money in his bank yet.

Valero did a quick mental calculation and concluded that the figure Dallis had dealt with must be about five million Euros. The very amount that had gone missing when Kidd and the Irishman got incinerated. He had initially thought that the money may have been on the boat, but his doubts were raised after he had managed to get one of the Marina staff to look at the CCTV and it was clear that the yacht had never entered the harbour.

Therefore, it was likely that someone had the money. He didn't know if Dallis had already received the money as he had just mentioned an 'enquiry'. It wasn't a large amount, from the perspective of the agent of a drugs empire controlling billions, but this was his 'bit on the side' money he was using to feather his own nest rather than pass it back to Caracas. In any case, an example had to be made. And the money could easily still be on the Island of Tenerife.

When he returned to La Gomera, Valero set about making discreet enquiries. There were several people on Tenerife who were capable of making the Vatican City connection: Valdez, from Santa Cruz, Montero, from La Laguna and Cabrera, the sweaty guy from the south of the island.

Valera checked with a contact at the airport. There was a regular flight direct from Tenerife Sud to Rome. A few weeks after the yacht caught fire, Guillermo Cabrera had flown out on the 0830 plane, returning the next day.

***

Isabella Cabrera was a large woman, in the way that Tenerifian women are. Brought up on a diet of fish, rabbit, Paella and

Canarian potatoes, she was big in the areas that mattered. A large backside was complemented by an ample bosom, she was heavy but shapely, her olive skin set off by beautiful black hair.

There had been three kidnappers. Her four children were at school and she was busy in her kitchen when they arrived. Entering by a rear door, they seized her. One, she disabled by a well-directed kick to the groin. Another was hit in the face by a cast iron Paella dish. Despite her efforts, they managed to apply chloroform, bung her into the boot of the car and transport her to a secluded beach, where they humped her onto a motorboat and carted her off to incarceration in La Gomera.

I met Guillermo outside the Duck. He was frantic. He had received a message from the kidnappers, stating they had his wife. He returned home and found the kitchen in chaos. Then he received a further message where the caller stated: 'we know you have the cash. You have forty-eight hours to get it to us or the fat bitch dies.'

'That's the problem, Danny – we can't get the cash. It means going to Rome. The rigmarole it needs to close the accounts and gather the money – it could take weeks.'

'Call the cops, tell them everything. I'm not bothered. I'll take the rap. I'll tell them I gave you the money after a big win in a London casino – it's thin, but it should keep you out of jail. Fuck it, I'll just fess up.' I delved in my pocket for my phone.

'Danny, wait. I'll make one phone call first.' Guillermo got out his mobile and dialled a number. I could make out a female voice on the other end. They talked in Spanish, her tone of voice gradually changing from concern to worry, then absolute fury. Cabrera turned the phone off and put it in his pocket.

'Who was that?' I asked.

'Her sister – she is on her way.'

Fifteen minutes later, a black Alfa Romeo screeched to a halt outside the Duck.

Out stepped Ellen Perez, who in addition to being the leading female investigator on the island, was the welfare representative of the local Guardia Civil and, apparently, the sister of the kidnapped Isabella Cabrera.

She flew at Guillermo, casting an eye at me, rattling away in Spanish at Cabrera. Checking herself, she fixed me with a piercing glare.

'What have you got to do with this?'

'It my fault, Ellen – I'm truly sorry,'

She spat out a curse in Spanish. Guillermo tried to placate his sister-in-law and wrestle with his own panic at the same time. Eventually, they seemed to come to a decision.

Ellen took the lead.

'Look, there is no point in an action that will either lead to my sister's death or my brother-in-law going to prison. He tells me you can't get the cash in time.'

I looked at her. In my earphones, Al Martino sang 'Spanish Eyes'. *Not now, Al, not now.*

'Con them – tell them they can have the money in twenty-four hours – tell them the English cripple has the cash. Tell them they will have no trouble – he will be glad to be rid of it,' I said.

Ellen listened to me. She was a good woman and a good cop, but where her family was concerned, she was prepared to do anything to protect them.

First, she wanted her sister safe. Then she wanted to make sure that Guillermo got a pass on any prosecution. She wanted her sister's family and way of life protected as well. Her contempt for me as author of all her family's trouble was palpable, but she was also pragmatic enough to know that she needed me to play my part in Isabella's rescue.

Cabrera spoke to the kidnappers. He spun them a line about this brain-damaged, crippled English guy who had the cash. It was true that he was trying to help the Englishman to launder the money, but the guy was so goofy, he still had the cash with him, or at the very least he knew where it was. Basically, they had to get the Englishman. In return, he wanted his wife back.

***

Edwin Valero had been a gangster since he was a child. Brought up by a single mother in the backstreets of Caracas, he had done well at school until he fell into the clutches of 'The Cartel of the Suns', the military-ran, heavily armed organization that runs the drug trade in Venezuela and beyond. Initially a local drug runner, he had become a trusted overseer, and his knowledge of the rat-runs of Caracas proved useful.

A resourceful manager, eventually he was promoted, and was assigned a new position in charge of the Canarian interests of the cartel. As well as supplying the coke so popular with the tourists, Valero used the drug profits to invest in restaurants, hotels, and the construction industry.

More recently, however, he had personally diversified into the illegal 'blood' diamonds trade, because the Canaries were so convenient for the West African-based traders. This cash he kept. It was an irregular and unreliable income stream, and as the money he returned to his masters was regular and reliable, it was the latter to which he devoted his considerable energies.

Valero had a small team of Venezuelans, loyal to him, spread throughout the Islands. They were generally low key, operating under the local law enforcement's radar, bribing and intimidating if absolutely necessary but more motivated by ongoing income than any macho empire building.

At his castle HQ in La Gomera, Valero's ex-military hardmen were able to respond to any of the issues confronting the

Canarian network. They were mostly needed to protect the millions in cash and drugs stashed in the labyrinthine cellars situated under the old fortress he had converted into a luxury home. His castle overlooked the entrance to Vueltas, the port of Valle Gran Rey. The cellars were also where the kidnapped Isabella Cabrera had been taken.

Valero had slipped up – by entering into an arrangement with the Gringo Grant Kidd, he had broken the golden rule: don't use anyone but Venezuelans. You could trust Columbians if you had to, but you could never trust Gringoes. The Moroccans were customers, reliable regular payers, but kept at operational arm's length.

Kidd had delivered on several small bits of business, and Valero had decided that he could trust him. But the last time had been a disaster. The American smuggler had been given five million Euros to sail to Port Loko in Sierra Leone. While there, he was to collect and pay for a consignment of illegal blood diamonds. But Kidd missed the transfer point, making a complete balls-up of the job. And when he eventually made contact with the seller, he showed himself up as such a total arsehole that the seller came to the conclusion that Kidd was a CIA plant. Valero had tried to re-establish contact but, the seller was spooked and ran for cover.

Valero ordered Kidd to return to La Gomera with the money. When he got back to the Canaries, Kidd put in at

Tenerife and paid off his small crew. He then dumped the money with someone who would stay quiet.

Then Kidd had to face Valero and his minders. He had more chance of surviving the encounter if the money was left in a safe place rather than brought with him. It was Kidd's gambling chip and he played it well.

***

After he left me at my apartment that morning, Kidd had gathered Shaun to help him crew the yacht across. He withstood the fury of Valero and made his apologies. As peace was restored, they discussed how they were to rekindle the deal with the Sierra Leoneans. This eventually led to a telephone conversation with Kidd apologizing to the illegal diamond dealers. Arrangements were made to reinstate the trade and a date was set for two weeks ahead.

Valero wanted the money back for safekeeping and Kidd was happy to see the back of it for a while. After a long dinner and thanking his lucky stars that he had not incurred the wrath of the Venezuelans, he set off back to the Marina, promising to return with the cash the next day.

Unfortunately, unbeknown to anyone, the propane gas bottle stored in the galley was leaking. Whether or not one of them lit a cigarette or tried to light the gas cooker in the cabin, no one knows. In any case, it exploded, killing them both in the fireball.

***

While we were plotting her escape, Isabella Cabrera was doing her bit. Locked in a small room in the castle's cellars, she was kicking up a storm.

After coming round from the chloroform, she had bided her time and when one of her guards came to check on her, she waited as he lent over her prone body and bit off the top of his ear. By the time he had retreated to the door, she had scratched his face and kicked him in the goolies.

From then on, the hard-men fed her by sliding food under the door. They called her *mujer malvada* (devil woman), and the tough Venezuelans ruefully decided that it would have been a better idea to kidnap one of her kids.

As soon as Cabrera got in contact with them, a swap was arranged. In return for his wife, Cabrera would guide the gangsters to the Englishman. Once they were satisfied that he either had the cash or knew where it was, Isabella would be released.

***

Ellen agreed to my plan.

'What do you need from me?' she asked.

'Can you get some firepower? We need guns.'

'I'll see what I can do.' Ellen sighed, and I couldn't look her in the eye as I visualized the implications if she got caught.

I had caused this. A good woman's career was on the line. I should have told her about the money in the first place. Ellen would be lucky to escape jail because of this.

In my ears, The Temptations were singing 'Don't Leave Me This Way' as she walked back to the Alfa. 'Can't Get Next to You' would have been equally appropriate.

***

The found property office in Santa Cruz Police HQ was shared with the evidence storage facility. Inevitably, it contained the tools of the trade for virtually every criminal enterprise.

Jorge, the old cop who managed the facility was a good friend of Ellen's. She had represented him when the administrators wanted to pension him off. Jorge considered himself firmly in her debt. When she asked him to take a fifteen-minute break from his desk, he was surprised, but he could see that she needed a little help. She seemed upset about something.

With Jorge gone, Ellen took three semi-automatics, a machine pistol, enough ammunition to sustain a short war, and two kilos of high-grade cocaine. She placed everything in a large sports bag.

Jorge returned to his post, and Ellen assured him she would be back within twenty-four hours. Jorge told her not to rush, with a wink. The found property office's records weren't brilliant and Jorge set about covering his and Ellen's tracks in the paperwork.

Chapter Nine

That night, I went into the Duck. The northerners were in. I bought them drinks and took them to one side.

'How's business?' I asked.

'Good, Danny. We could always do a bit more but we're OK,' Gary said.

'How does £2,000 each sound for one night's work?'

'It's sounds fucking illegal, Danny, but the money sounds good,' Steve said.

'Two grand would be nice,' Gary agreed.

'So who do ya want killing?' asked Matt, the Yorkie.

I didn't go into any detail about the money. I just told them that Cabrera's wife had been kidnapped and that I was to be traded for her, but that I didn't want to go.

'Who the fuck's kidnapped her? It'd be like kidnapping Godzilla,' Gary sniggered. Apparently, they'd done some building work at the Cabreras' house.

'She's a scary bitch,' Steve commented.

'I like her,' said Yorkie a little dreamily, with an expression that caused both his mates to contemplate the weirdness of all things Yorkshire.

They were in. A "monkey" each in advance showed them I was serious.

***

Cabrera phoned. It was on. At 9pm the following night, a motorboat would enter the harbour and tie up. The mooring would be reserved, Cabrera would be waiting in his car and he would drive several Venezuelans to my villa. Once either me or the money were secured, Mrs Cabrera would be released.

I spoke to Ronnie and Wendy. They had worked out that something was up with me and Cabrera. They had bought a small boat for themselves out of the profits at the Duck and I told them I might need it, and them, for a little job after closing time. In the buccaneering spirit of the Tenerifian expat community, they agreed, smiling.

I retreated to the villa. I got out the wheelchair I hadn't used for months and sat facing the double doors leading from the rear entrance. I'd told Cabrera to use that entrance to bring the gangsters in. Covering my lower half was a tartan blanket. I looked like the invalid I'd been when I'd arrived on the island.

But under the blanket was an old Russian Stechkin machine pistol, supplied by Ellen Perez. It was cleaned, loaded and ready for action. I had attended a couple of firearms courses in the cops and I was confident that I could use this extremely deadly bit of kit if I needed to.

Ellen was to stay close to the Marina. The Mancs, Gary and Steve, had both been given their duties, also near the boat.

Meanwhile in the garage of my villa, armed with a Brooklyn Slugger baseball bat and a meat cleaver, was a big fat Yorkshireman with a penchant for insane violence, learned on the terraces of Elland Road, honed by the British Army, and also, apparently, a love for big domineering women.

***

The motorboat cruised slowly into the marina entrance. It was quiet now, the fishing crews either already ashore or starting to settle down, preparing for tomorrow's early start.

Cabrera stood next to his Jeep 4x4, nervously shifting from foot to foot. Despite the coolness of the evening, he was sweating profusely. Edwin Valero and members of his gang stood on the deck and as the boat docked, threw a line to Cabrera. One of his men jumped ashore and secured the boat at the other end.

Valero and two others left the boat and with the first man, joined Cabrera, four in total. Valero beckoned Cabrera to a porthole and Cabrera looked through see his beloved Isabella, handcuffed and muzzled, with two men on each side of her. One of them was holding a gun to her head. When she saw Cabrera, her expression changed from one of seething anger to absolute fury. Cabrera shuddered, but rescuing Isabella was his sole mission; he would worry about her retribution later.

Meanwhile, at the other end of the Marina, two men, originally from the Moss Side area of Manchester, clad in diving suits, silently slipped into the quiet waters of the Marina San Miguel.

Cabrera and the gangsters got into the 4x4 and set off for my villa.

***

The 4x4 pulled into my drive and as instructed, Cabrera brought them to the rear of the property. He opened the sliding double doors and entered. I sat facing them, between the doors, with the TV to my left. Anyone would think I was watching TV.

The four Venezuelans followed Cabrera in and fanned out across the room. I smiled a vacant smile and adjusted my wheelchair to face Cabrera. Valero spoke to someone on a two-way radio in Spanish. 'We have him,' I think he said.

'Danny, these men have come to collect the money you are looking after.'

'Oh, that's good.' I looked back to the TV.

'Where is it, Danny?'

Not taking my eyes from the screen, I pointed.

'In the cupboard behind the TV.'

The men all looked to my left. As they took their eyes off me, I dropped the blanket and fired a short burst into the ceiling above their heads.

I saw Valero go for a gun, but before he could reach it, a screaming banshee wearing a Leeds United away top stampeded into the room and with a scream loud enough to waken the dead, brought the Brooklyn Slugger down on the Venezuelan's head.

One of the others produced a gun. I levelled the machine pistol, but Cabrera beat me to it. A meaty right-hander connected to the point of the gunman's chin. He went down, tried to rise. Yorkie wielded the Brooklyn Slugger and connected with the back of his head. Another gunman wouldn't be on his feet for a while.

Two to go, both in my line of fire. Shock on their faces dawned as they realised I wasn't quite the drooling fool they were told about. Their hands went up.

'Kneel,' I told them. Their leader, Valero, was totally unconscious, as was one of their *companiones*.

Yorkie searched them: a knife, a razor, no firepower. He gave each of them a whack on the shins with the bat, just to keep them focused.

Cabrera picked up the leader's radio.

'On way,' he said, in his best attempt at a Venezuelan accent.

We tie-wrapped and gagged all four prisoners, divided them between us into two cars and headed off to the Marina.

***

Back on the quayside, a full-bodied Tenerifian woman, in a short skirt and low-cut, revealing blouse, was promenading along the walkway next to the moored boats. She was chewing gum and eyeing the decks, apparently a woman of the night-soliciting business. In fact, she was Ellen Perez, an officer of the Guardia Civil, using the skills she had learned working as a decoy for the Vice squad in Santa Cruz and Madrid.

The Venezuelans on the boat had relaxed a little after learning their plan had worked out and their amigos were returning. Soon they would be rid of this *perra horrible* and could get back to normal: dealing drugs, committing crime and making money. They all got together to eye the *prostituta* flaunting herself on the walkway.

In what was surely the first water-born attack by football hooligans, two members of the Manchester City Guvnors climbed up the side of the boat. Mrs Cabrera saw them and believed that despite her husbands' shortcomings, he had hired James Bond and his mate to release her.

The operation was made easier for the attackers by Mrs Cabrera joining in with gusto. She secured one of her captors around his neck, the chain of her handcuffs, squashing his throat.

He was a wiry man, but she was a big woman. He worked out in the gym, but she worked out in the kitchen and with the kids. Therefore, she was fitter than him.

The trio were soon joined, to the surprise of the Mancs as well as the bad guys, by a prostitute with a Glock pistol. She seemed to know the prisoner. Violence ensued – over-the-top, vengeful violence. It was over in a couple of minutes.

Their victory complete, they secured the bad guys and awaited developments. The Mancs eyed their female tag-team partners with interest.

The younger woman undid the handcuffs and removed the gag from her sister's mouth, who sighed with relief. They were big women, rounded in the right places, with lovely teeth, and oh, that hair. Gary and Steve recognised the older woman from that building job on her house.

'Muchas Gracias, Senor Bond,' she said, with a winning smile. Maybe their fat Yorkshireman friend was right about her after all.

***

Masca is a small village, lying at an altitude of 650 metres, in the Macizo de Teno mountains, some miles inland from the coast of Tenerife. It is frequently visited for its views and as a starting point for a four-hour downhill traverse to the sea by enthusiastic walkers. Beautiful during the hours of daylight, it is, at night, somewhat eerie.

It was certainly eerie if you were a tough guy and all your preconceptions about terrorizing people had been challenged in one night. When you didn't know where you were, and you and your companions were barely conscious and throbbing with pain.

And the people who had driven you to defeat and humiliation were two frogmen, a huge man in a Leeds United shirt, a prostitute with a pistol; her sister – a living nightmare; a sweaty, fat lawyer who could, when necessary, punch like a mule and was now sporting a *pistola*; and a guy with a speech defect and such a bad limp he needed a walking stick.

The Venezuelans had been stripped naked. Mr Cabrera, long released, was exacting retribution on her former captors at every opportunity, while castigating and kissing her husband at the same time.

I told them to start walking towards the sea, and that if they turned back, Mrs Cabrera would be waiting with a gun, and that a boat would meet them at the bottom of the trail.

We were making up this last bit of the plan as we went along. I was surprised we had got this far. Leaving the Cabreras with the machine pistol at the top of the trail, to ensure the gangsters didn't return, the rest of us returned to the Marina.

Ellen took the drugs she had liberated from the Police stores and passed them to the Mancs with instructions to hide them on the Venezuelans' boat. Then she made a phone call.

Steve the Manc was surprisingly good at piloting the boat, and, with Ronnie and Wendy following in their boat, we piloted the Venezuelans' yacht to the towering cliffs of the Playa de Masca.

We anchored the boat close to shore, jumped over to Ronnie and Wendy's boat and waited, hidden behind a rocky outcrop.

As dawn broke, the Venezuelans appeared, stark naked and sore-footed. They carried one man who seemed to be slipping in and out of consciousness. They looked surprised to see their own boat bobbing around in the bay.

They swam from the beach and boarded their boat. Almost immediately, they set off towards La Gomera, a short but bumpy trip. Halfway across, they were intercepted by a Guardia Civil patrol boat, acting on an apparently anonymous tip off.

A search of the boat revealed two kilo packs of white powder. Unknown to the arresting Guardia Officers, they had been planted there earlier on the instructions of Ellen Perez, who had correctly suspected them to be cocaine.

As all the occupants of the boat were naked at the time of arrest, they were arrested for the possession of drugs and on a charge of outraging public morals.

The cops raided the castle in La Gomera the same morning. The raid was led by Senior Investigator Ellen Perez. Further arrests were made, and large amounts of money, drugs and arms were seized. Serious charges were made and the prisoners were all shipped off to high security remand prisons in Toledo.

Part Two

Chapter Ten

Months went by. The Venezuelans, now subject to the notoriously slow Spanish judicial system, were well-tucked out of the way.

I was enjoying my life, and the daily physio and gym were making me healthy and strong. In the gym, I had met Aagesh, a Tamil who owned a restaurant on the island which specialised in South Asian food. He was an exponent of Tamil stick fighting, and I started to do some workouts with him.

My knees were getting better, but they were never going to fully recover. My training with Aagesh, combined with my ever-present African hardwood walking stick, helped to ensure that just in case of unexpected retribution, I would be able to look after myself.

Ellen had experienced some difficulty in replacing the guns in the Police evidence room, as Jorge, the clerk in charge, had doctored the manifest to save her the trouble. So I agreed to hang on to the old Russian machine pistol and one of the Glocks. I kept the Glock in the safe at the Duck and hid the Stechkin in the garden at my villa.

My continual background music continued. It seemed that tinnitus was going to be my long-term companion, but the music really helped, and I was becoming something of an expert on jazz, Motown and my favourite, the blues.

Nights were spent in the Tame Duck, which was getting busier by the month. It was becoming the place to visit, whether you were a resident or were taking a holiday in the Golf del Sur, Amarilla or were in the area of Miguel St Abona.

The pub opened at nine am, serving full English breakfasts as well as catering for the croissant and coffee set. Lunch had become popular, once Ronnie convinced the best pancake maker on the island to join us and run the place until 6pm, when the evening menu kicked in with great steaks, pastas, and locally sourced seafood.

Wendy was in her element. She hired excellent bar and kitchen staff, who were paid well. Ronnie's initiative in opening a smaller bar at the rear of the main area, creating an area for drinkers and smokers, had also paid off. We catered for everyone.

At 9pm, the music started, and with Ronnie and Wendy's reputation, we were able to attract some of the best entertainers on the island.

I had started to drive again, albeit I could only manage in an automatic. The range of movement in my knees had improved but operating a clutch with my weakest knee was still a bit much.

Wendy missed paying a couple of small utility bills on time and we received red letters demanding payment. To save time,

I offered to drive to the council office in El Médano to pay them.

I hadn't travelled much beyond Golf del Sur since my arrival. When I did, I tended to go to Los Christianos and the other towns down the coast. I needed some clothes, so I took the opportunity to get to know El Médano and take a look around the shops; basically, to have a half-day change of scene and get a couple of bills paid.

As I drove out of Golf del Sur, I became aware of a black Isuzu pickup truck behind me. It contained two men wearing sunglasses. They looked North African, not Spanish, and they maintained a good distance behind me, but were still there as I drove along the backroads and headed for El Medano.

On reaching the town, I parked near the walkway and strolled back into the main shopping area. There was no sign of the pickup. The town was busy, and I entered a men's clothing store where I bought a few shirts, a couple of pairs of trousers, a pair of Nike trainers and some socks and briefs. I went back to the car, put all my purchases in the boot and set off to the council offices to pay the bills.

I saw the Isuzu again, slowly driving down the main street. It was quartering the town. They were looking for someone, and as they had followed me from Golf del Sur, it was a fairly safe bet that it was me.

I paid the bills, then walked back towards my car. I decided to observe my vehicle from a distance for a while, just in case the two guys in the pickup showed up and were interested in it. I found a café overlooking the car park, got a coffee and waited.

After about ten minutes, the Isuzu crawled alongside my car and the driver took a long look inside. He then parked in the row behind my car and waited.

The sirens could be heard in the distance and they were getting closer. My phone rang. It was Ellen Perez.

'Danny – in a few moments, police cars will be in the area where you are drinking coffee and armed officers will be obvious in the street. I will pull up in my Alfa outside the café. As soon as I stop, you are to quickly get into the back seat.'

Van Morrison was singing 'Ride on Josephine'. *Ride on, Ellen. I don't know what's going on, but clearly you do.*

The fact that the cops were watching me would normally be a worry, but in these circumstances, I was relieved.

I knew better than to ask questions. I readied myself, and as the sirens drew closer, I saw two armed response vehicles surround the Isuzu. The driver and passenger raised their hands, were dragged out and placed face-first on the tarmac.

As they hit the ground, Ellen's car flew around the corner. Obeying orders, as I was incapable of running, I walked as fast as my bad knees would allow and threw myself into the back of the Alfa.

We drove off at high speed with another armed response vehicle following us. Soon we were in the foothills of Mount Teide, the huge volcano that dominates the island of Tenerife. After a few miles, Ellen told the accompanying car to leave us. We pulled into an isolated restaurant and parked at the rear of the building.

Ellen beckoned me to get out of the back seat and I followed her to the rear entrance. There were a few cars and motorbikes parked at the front of the restaurant, and some cyclists taking a break from the wicked climb to the top of the mountain.

The rear of the restaurant was occupied by two men. Suits: investigators – senior suits. In my headphones, Enrico Morricone was playing the title theme from the Untouchables. Never was my musical background more apt.

***

Coronel Paulino Uzcudzen had been a cop for over twenty-five years. A Basque, he made his name fighting terrorists in his native region before transferring to Madrid and the Serious Organized Crime section of the Guardia. After a period attached to the FBI, he had completed the FBI senior agents' course at Quantico and worked for a year with the Met in London, attached to their drug squad.

He was intelligent, yet forceful; loved or feared by those who worked under him. He had transferred to the Canaries to take charge of the local detective force after a period of weak management had led to poor detection results, apathy, and corruption.

He had swept through the department like a tornado, sacking and where possible, prosecuting the corrupt, demoting or forcing into retirement the inept and idle; the decent, honest cops loved it.

***

'You are under arrest. Would you like a coffee?' His first words to me were accompanied by a broad smile.

Trying to sort out my thoughts and trying to mentally list the myriad offences I was guilty of, I asked the obvious question.

'What for? Yes, I would like a coffee.'

Uzcudzen laughed. 'Where should I start? Is café con leche OK? I know you Brits love your milk.'

He asked his companion if he would do the honours and he disappeared around the end of the serving area. Ellen sat down next to the most senior detective in the Canary Islands.

'Maybe charges relating to the Russian machine pistol in your villa or the Glock you have hidden somewhere that we would no doubt find if we raided the Duck. More probably, if I set our financial investigators onto the sources of your money... By the way, Senor Cabrera will tell us whatever we want to know if we ask him – we have as much on him as we have on you, we just haven't had that conversation yet. Whether we do is subject to the answers you give me in this conversation.'

I gulped, and sat back in the chair. This guy was good.

'Regarding Ellen, I know what she did. I know why she did it – nothing is going to happen to her, because she told me what she had done. She was wrong to do it, but I would have done exactly the same in her position. If you try to implicate her, then when we search your villa or the Duck, large amounts of class A drugs are going to mysteriously appear.' Through this, he never stopped smiling.

'What do you want from me?'

'The men following you today are from a Moroccan crime cartel from based in Marrakesh. They are associates of the Venezuelans you are responsible for imprisoning. Your actions have led to serious damage to their plans. They are here to get their money if possible, but mostly to kill you in a very gruesome way.

He went on to inform me that the Moroccans wrongly believed, through lawyers representing the imprisoned Venezuelans, that the five million Euros was still in play in Tenerife.

The men who were arrested today after following me to El Medano had been told to find either me, the money or both. If they couldn't find the money, they would just kill me.

One way or the other, I was screwed again. A dangerous criminal gang was after me, and the most effective detective in the Spanish legal system had me. Still, the coffee was good.

Gravel voiced James Carruthers was singing 'Colt 45' in my headphones. *Sounds as though another firearm might come in handy right now, James.*

The meeting went on for an hour or so. Uzcudzen told me how much trouble I was in and outlined what life was like in the Spanish prison system. I assured him I was willing to do anything that would keep me out of the clink.

Uzcudzen's instructions to me were clear. The immediate danger was over: the two hitmen were in custody, not in a normal facility but one I was due to become familiar with.

Chapter Eleven

Reina Sofia airport, equally well-known as Tenerife South, is an international airport, largely serving the tourist trade of around eleven million visitors per year. Within its curtilage is a remand facility for persons being deported from the island.

Beneath that is a further suite of rooms used by the Spanish authorities to hold dangerous prisoners they wish to segregate from the general prisoner population. Occasionally, the suite is used by other authorities such as the United States, DEA, FBI and CIA. MI6 and the French security services are also occasional tenants.

The prisoners are usually there for intensive interrogation, including members of ISIS, Taliban, Al Qaeda, and leading members of the drug cartels.

Usually, an unmarked private jet is directed to a berthing point near to the facility and the prisoner, accompanied by his or her interrogators, is quickly banged-up in the interrogation suite.

The process is intense and usually lasts little more than a week. After that time, if the interrogators are any good, they will have broken the most difficult prisoner. Information received, the prisoner will be again placed into a private jet and whisked to whichever jurisdiction is dealing with him.

If not broken, the prisoner could then be taken to even more remote suites in Romania or North Africa to continue their "debrief".

The prisoners never even know which country they're in. There's no judicial oversight, and few politicians are aware of these interrogations.

The Canarian government is paid a great deal of money for this service by democratic governments wishing to sidestep their own touchy-feely legal systems and the attention of Human Rights lawyers.

***

Two days after we'd met in the restaurant, Uzcudzen led me into this suite. I had studied the script he had given me, which laid out exactly what was expected of me. The room was luxurious: mahogany desk, bookshelves, nice carpets, and rugs. I sat in my appointed seat, facing the door through which a blindfolded, handcuffed man was led.

I recognized him as the driver of the 4x4 that had tailed me and who I last saw being handcuffed in the car park in El Medano. He had large headphones on, suppressing all sensory input. The men handling him were in plain clothes. I knew they must be cops or Spanish security agents. God knows what the prisoner thought of them.

The prisoner was seated opposite me and secured into place before the headphones and the blindfolds were removed. I sat behind my posh desk. He had been identified by the profiler as the weaker of the two.

'What is your name?' I asked. He blinked and looked around in confusion.

'What is your name?' I repeated.

'Anjum.'

'Where are you from?'

'I want a lawyer.'

The slap came from the giant cop standing behind him. I pointed to the cop.

'He is your lawyer,' I told him. 'And by the way, I am not a Police Officer. Your situation is not hopeless – your friend unfortunately was not co-operative, and his body is awaiting disposal. You have the option of life.'

'Who are you?'

'I'm the man you came to kill. Surely you recognize me?'

Seeing me in this luxurious office, surrounded by bodyguards, caused him to rethink his situation.

'Where are the cops?'

'I own the cops. Next question.'

He gulped. I told the cops to release his handcuffs. He was given a bottle of water.

'I gave your friend the opportunity to help us, please watch this,'

Using a remote control, I turned on a TV that was fixed to the wall. A video came on of a man being water-boarded, beaten, and subjected to electric shocks. Eventually a torturer was heard to say: 'I've gone too far, he's dead.'

It was horrible; as horrible as the CIA-trained technicians could mock-up such a scene using CGI. It looked horrific. It had never happened.

Anjum thought it had.

'You will either talk to me or you are next.'

'What do you want to know?'

Uzcudzen and Ellen had been watching through a one-way mirror. Now, they entered the room and sat quietly at the back of the room. Ellen was taking notes, with Uzcudzen listening intently.

'Who sent you?'

'Abdel Kadar.'

I saw Uzcudzen look up. Ellen started writing. Clearly the name meant something.

'Why?'

'He told us you'd got his associates arrested and stole money from him.'

'How much were you paid?'

'Five grand each up front. Another five grand each on completion.'

Compared to what I'd been offered for just sitting on the money for twelve hours, these lads worked cheap.

'What were you to do if you found the money?'

'Phone a number he gave me.'

'Where's the number?'

'It's in my phone.'

A cop passed him his phone. He scrolled down and pointed at the number on the screen. 'That's him.'

'OK, here's my offer. You talk to these guys,' he said, indicating the cops. 'And I'll let you live. If you lie, or in any way fuck around, we will do to you what we did to your mate. Talk and live, or die screaming – up to you.'

I walked out.

Uzcudzen stood and joined me. He beckoned Ellen to follow him and we left the room. They were impressed by my performance. I hoped to God that it would buy me some brownie points – I was going to need them.

The shooter was re-handcuffed. The gag and blindfold were reinstated, and the earphones were put back on. The prisoner went back to the solitary confinement he'd come from.

I was told to go home and stay there. I had picked up my car from El Medano the previous day. I drove from the airport back to the Duck, where I had a couple of overlarge Johnny

Walker Black labels, before doing as I was told, isolating myself in the villa.

The phone rang early the next morning.

It was Ellen. She was friendly enough; brisk and business-like. I had conned her and her colleagues when I first met them. I'd never really had the chance to explain to her that I was in a no-win situation regarding Shaun, Grant and the money when we'd first met.

I'd been in such dire health when I'd arrived in Tenerife, and I'd improved so fast I'd surprised myself. Ellen would have difficulty believing that I'd been such a mumbling, stumbling wreck.

I liked Ellen a lot; she was a lovely woman, also conscientious and basically honest. But I had created a situation where her professionality had been compromised and I thought she hated me for it. I didn't blame her. I was wrong.

Ellen told me to make sure I stayed in the villa. They thought they had all the hitmen in custody, but weren't sure – they had plain clothes cops in the area and she and Uzcudzen would be coming to see me next day.

It was mid-afternoon when I saw the Alfa coming down the road. I started to make coffee. If I was about to get locked up, I may as well have a last decent cup and show some courtesy to Uzcudzen and Ellen. After all, they had saved me from a grisly end.

They came in and I handed them their coffee. They took a seat on the high stools that were placed alongside the breakfast bar.

Paulino Uzcudzen sipped his coffee. He wore a nice Gucci suit. He looked comfortable in it: power suit, powerful man.

'OK Danny, this is the situation. Since you convinced Anjum that you 'own' the local Guardia Civil, he has been singing like a bird. At six am yesterday morning, the other would-be assassin was shown the video of Anjum making his statement and decided to join in – an attempt to make sure he doesn't get all the blame for the botched assassination job on you.'

Uzcudzen took a sip of coffee and continued.

'Anjum still thinks we have killed his partner. They have separately implicated senior members of the Moroccan Kadar cartel in a conspiracy to kill you. They have also divulged various other serious criminal activities that Kadar is involved in – the evidence looks very good.'

I nodded, and the senior investigator stared back at me with a smile playing on his face.

'One hour ago, I received a call from The Royal Moroccan Gendarmerie in Rabat. They arrested senior members of the Kadar crime organization about three hours ago, at the request of the Spanish Interior ministry. They've all been placed on a specially chartered plane and will be in jail in Madrid this evening. They will not get to trial for at least two years. Even if they are found not guilty, their criminal enterprise is badly damaged.'

'Where does this leave me?'

'I have thought long and hard about this, Danny. It leaves you here, in sunny Golf del Sur, enjoying the sun, spending your money, keeping a low profile, and getting your health back. Cabrera told us that your first instinct when his wife was taken was to hand yourself in. Later you offered yourself in a hostage swap and faced down four killers from a wheelchair. That means something to me, and I know it means a lot to Ellen.'

Ellen smiled shyly. Maybe she thought a little better of me than I suspected.

'Stick around, Danny. Someone like you in the English-speaking community could be valuable to me. Maybe, in the future, we can work together again.'

The relief was massive. Not only was I a free man, I got to keep the money. I sipped my coffee, Ellen smiled right at me. *Oh, that hair.*

In my ears, Joe Cocker was singing 'With a little help from my friends'. *Yes, Joe, and after a few crap years, it appears I have some.*

Chapter Twelve

Peace had returned to Golf del Sur. The Cabrera family got back to normal, with Guillermo the caring father and solicitous spouse and Isabella the loving parent. She was now a little more tolerant of her husband's shortcomings, following his heroics on her behalf with the Venezuelans.

Those same Venezuelans who now languished in Toledo supermax jail and were still about two years from facing trial.

One lunchtime, I was sitting outside the Tame Duck, drinking coffee. A couple of locals were playing pool inside. The holidaymakers were promenading as usual, mostly making their way to the small weekly market that was held on the car park near to the four-star Aquamarina hotel.

Cabrera arrived, in his usual linen suit, panama hat; his belly protruding over his trousers and his shirt struggling to keep fastened. He was sweaty even when relaxed, the sweat running off his forehead and into his large black moustache, causing it to gleam. He sat down and I ordered him a coffee.

'Danny, I have something on my mind and I want to discuss it with you.'

'I'm all ears.'

The look of incomprehension on his face led me to change my response.

'I'm listening, Guillermo.'

I liked him a lot. He was a tricky customer, no doubt – a fraudster, money launderer and all-round bad egg, but he loved his kids and he adored his fearsome wife, despite living in permanent fear of her. You've got to like a guy like that.

'I have to change my life. This latest escapade with Isabella has taught me that I cannot place my family in danger. I have a decent business in my legal practice. The other stuff has to go – I feel I want to branch out into the honest world instead of operating in the twilight.' He was quite emotional; the incident with the Venezuelans had rattled him badly.

'On this island, Danny, we have many people who sometimes need the services of a man like you. Your experience as a cop – a detective, can be useful. Often people go missing. Usually they turn up, but sometimes they do not.'

I nodded, listening carefully to his words. What was he getting at?

'I hear of people from Europe looking for a private eye to observe the activities of a wife or husband here for a spa holiday with the girls or a golf holiday with the boys. If we went into business together you could run that side of it while I helped out with any financial enquiries, anything that needed the eye of a man used to financial...how do you say? Pokery jiggery?'

'Jiggery pokery,' I corrected but I took his point.

Cabrera and Mclinden International Investigators? It had a ring to it, not exactly Holmes and Watson or Batman and Robin but it could work. I wasn't in any way short of money – the cash was rolling in from my 'investment' and from the Duck. I wasn't bored but running a bar wasn't really my thing and Ronnie and Wendy certainly didn't need me. Why not?

***

There was a small shop for rent at the front of the Edificio where my old apartment was, just opposite the Duck. It had been a few things: a pharmacy, and a hippyish boutique. It wasn't really big enough for retail, but it would make a nice office for me and occasionally Cabrera, maybe with a third desk for a buxom blonde secretary like those who worked for Philip Marlowe, Sam Spade or Mickey Spillane.

I had the equipment: a mobile phone, a laptop, sunglasses, a straw fedora. Useless at tech, we got a passing child to design and install our website and we were in business. I had insisted on changes: we were Mclinden and Cabrera, Sunset Investigations, London, Madrid, and Golf del Sur. Mostly Golf del Sur.

The office had one drawback: the glass front door. Because of its situation, it reflected images from inside very powerfully; it was as good as any mirror. I found myself looking at what I had become. I had been a strong, rugby-playing cop, who feared nothing and no one; the first one into a ruck or a punch-up, usually the last man standing. What I saw in the mirrored glass wasn't handsome, it wasn't ugly, but it was irreparably damaged.

I had become hunched. Two years of being in wheelchair, followed by crutches and now a stick, had created a roundness to my shoulders. The scar running from my scalp into my forehead was livid where they had operated to stop my brain bleed. Standing up was less of an effort than it had been, if I didn't sit down for too long – then my knees seized up. I cured my feelings of mild depression caused by looking at myself too often. I put blinds up.

I worked out daily. The stick fighting routine really helped. I was never going to progress to a high level, but when I didn't visit the dojo, I went to the gym. Every day I swam. Progress was slow now, but if I kept the activity up, I felt I would not get worse. In my ears AC/DC gave way to ZZ Top on random selection with an absolute cornucopia of over 40,000 songs between them.

We got a few jobs, just as Cabrera said we would: a couple of tourists who had gone missing. One I found living in a drunken and drugged haze in a studio apartment and didn't realise he should be back in Belgium by now. Another one, a Swedish girl, had a history of depression and she had been seen one midnight walking towards the sea, where, next morning her shoes had been found in the sand. A tragic, long walk on a narrow beach was the only conclusion I could come to.

***

The Tame Duck was, as usual, busy. Ronnie had just introduced the Drifters, the great American vocal group. In fact, this was, at least the fiftieth incarnation of the Drifters operating worldwide. It was the third active incarnation on the Island, to accompany the numerous tribute bands celebrating Elvis, Rod Stewart, Elton John, Neil Diamond and the Beatles.

These kinds of bands provide night-in, night-out nostalgia to the middle aged and elderly, amusement to the young, and money in the tills of the bars that employ them.

The difference was that Ronnie knew who was good, not so good and rubbish. We always got the good ones – we paid more, got the best bands, and got the bar full.

I was sitting at the bar, as usual. I had cut down on the hard stuff and contented myself with either a few cold beers, a nice local wine or a Rioja. I was in good form, fit and tanned.

I had been spending more time with Ellen Perez. Funny how helping the cops to put away a dangerous international gang and rescuing Ellen's sister from kidnappers had brought us together. But now Ellen had been promoted and transferred to Barcelona. As her home and family were in Tenerife, she returned home from time to time. I missed her, but the new business was keeping me busy and motivated.

The Duck provided distractions. Even for a lame man with a speech defect, the many widows and divorcees that came to the area led to some interesting and sometimes energetic diversions, and it was not unknown for the maid to turn up for work in the morning at the villa to find an extra occupant.

***

It was June, one of those rare nights when the bar was a little quiet. Many of the silver surfers from northern Europe had gone home for their own country's summer, and it was too early for the summer holiday makers. Still, we had the regulars in and were ticking over nicely.

The door opened and in walked possibly the most beautiful woman I had ever seen. She was ebony black. Her skin was perfect, without a blemish; she was dressed in a white dress with a white pashmina. She was alone and appeared nervous as she approached the bar.

Ronnie was singing onstage. Wendy and the other two barmaids were busy at the far end of the bar. Our visitor stood alongside me as I sat on my usual stool.

'Are you Danny Mclinden?'

'Yes ma'am, can I help you?'

'I was told you would be here. I called at your office. A man called Guillermo told me where to find you.'

I checked my phone. I had a couple of missed calls from Cabrera. Because of the noise in the bar, my tinnitus was still limiting my hearing and I hadn't detected the trembling sensation of my phone vibrating.

'What can I do for you?'

'I think my sister may be in trouble and I'd like you to do some detective work for me.'

It was late. We normally got enquiries during office hours, but this lady was clearly troubled.

'Why don't we go over to my office where it's quieter and you can tell me what the problem is.'

I had a bottle of Vidonia Blanco on the go, and I grabbed a couple of glasses and the bottle before we walked the short distance to the office.

I sat behind my desk and she took the chair normally occupied by Cabrera. I poured us both a glass of white wine.

'What's your name?'

'I am Emilie Aise. I'm from Guadeloupe. I came to Europe about five years ago. I'm a singer – I've made a couple of records but I make a good living working on cruise lines and in the top end hotels in Europe and here on the islands. My sister Jessica is two years older than me. She's also a musician but classically trained – she followed me out here. She has worked with some top orchestras and as a session musician. Because we travel so much, we don't see each other a lot but we have an apartment here in Golf del Sur that we both use.'

She adjusted in the chair. A couple of sips of the wine had eased her nervousness. My infirmities being obvious, women felt I was no threat to them and seemed to relax easily with me.

She warmed to her story. Her beauty was enhanced by her voice: Caribbean with a French undertone. I would have listened to her all night if she had been reading the telephone directory.

'When I returned from working on a cruise ship about a week ago, I expected to find my sister in the apartment. Instead, there was no sign of her. She didn't answer her phone or reply to messages. When I asked a couple of neighbours, they said she'd been seeing an older guy, in his fifties, very well dressed, Range Rover – very distinguished-looking. After a couple of days, my phone went. It was Jessica. She apologized for not contacting me but said her phone wasn't working. She didn't sound right – she wouldn't tell me where she was, just that she was safe, was with a man who was helping her career, and that she would be in touch.'

'Maybe she's in love.'

'That's fine, but I know my sister. We're close – she would want to tell me. I just want to know where she is and that she's safe – also to find out who this man is.'

We finished the wine and arranged to meet the next morning at her apartment. I called a cab and watched her as she glided towards the opened door. I hobbled after her and reaching the office entrance, returned her wave as she drove away.

In my ears, Earl Klugh was playing 'Dr Macumba'. *Mysterious.*

Next morning, I drove to Emilie's apartment, which was in the luxurious development El Nautico, facing west, on the frontline of the ocean.

I parked in the street nearby and walked in, my stick tapping the pavement. I noticed the CCTV camera, which looked good quality. There was a security guard in the reception office. I could see the monitors – he had a perfect view of the car park and the surrounding area. I told him Emilie was expecting me, and he checked his list.

'Senor Maclinden?'

I nodded.

'Go straight in, Senor.'

I went to Emilie's door. I knocked and she let me in. Her earlier nervousness and worried look had gone, and she seemed pleased to see me. She looked stunning, wearing a gauzy dress over a skimpy swimming costume.

After inviting me in, she confirmed that her sister had not been in touch overnight. She told me that earlier that morning, she had made further enquiries with her nearest neighbours, but they could not add to the information she already had.

I asked her how well she knew the security guard.

'Pablo? Oh, he's lovely.'

'Go and ask him if you can see his recordings for the past few days. Tell him a friend thinks he may have had his car bumped in the car park and you wanted to help him find who had run into it. And say you think the driver who caused the damage was in a Range Rover.'

Emilie phoned Pablo the guard and asked him to find the car in his CCTV archives.

Fifteen minutes later, Pablo phoned.

'I have seen the car, senorita. It doesn't run into any other cars – your sister gets into that car. I'm sure she would have reported it had there been an accident.'

'Pablo, do you mind if I look?'

'No problema.'

We walked down to the reception. It was quiet and Pablo beckoned us into the small CCTV suite. He had freeze-framed the Range Rover and the occupants. Its registration number was also clearly in shot. I memorized it. Tenerife registered:

MME3242. In the footage, Jessica seemed relaxed. She appeared tall like her sister, maybe a few pounds heavier, very shapely and attractive, another stunner. Her companion was shorter than her, maybe 5ft 6 or 7. Slim, fit, well-heeled, wearing a light-blue designer suit. He had dark hair that was grey at temples, in his fifties. The recording was nearly a week old.

I asked Pablo for a printout. He looked at Emilie. She nodded, he printed; I gave him a twenty Euro note.

We returned to Emilie's apartment. She made coffee. We looked at the photo together.

'She seems OK – happy in fact,' Emilie said.

I was reminded of my time as a young cop, watching a CCTV recording of a young couple walking home together on a dark street after a night out. They were laughing and fooling around together. Anyone would have thought they were just a happy couple. Ten minutes later, he killed her. Images can belie what's really going on.

I left Emilie and returned to the office, promising to contact her once I had made headway.

***

Once back in Golf, I entered the office. Cabrera had gone home for lunch.

My earlier adventures in Tenerife had led me to forming a friendly acquaintance with Colonel Paulino Uzcudzen, Chief of Detectives on the islands. He had told me that one day he would like to use my talents. Now I was going to see if I could use his.

I phoned him.

'Hi Danny.' I was flattered that he had me on his phone's contacts list. 'How's the private detective business?'

'Paulino, I'm surprised you know about it. I'm just doing a few missing persons – Cabrera is chasing bad debts – nothing exciting, but it keeps us busy.'

He asked about my health and repeated his thanks for the help I had given him previously.

'I need a favour, Paulino.'

'I will if I can.'

'I need to know who a guy is. I've got a photo of him and a car registration number. Can you help?'

'It has to be good, Danny. I can't just let you have this kind of info without a good reason.'

I outlined the situation. Uzcudzen wanted the girl's details and I gave him what I had: names, approximate ages of the sister, their address, and their occupations. And a description of the guy and the registration number of his Range Rover.

'Give me a couple of hours, Danny.'

I killed the time by walking down to the Marina. There is a small café at the very end of the walkway that specializes in Tenerifian Barraquito coffee liqueurs and very cold beer. It was the latter that attracted me.

I tapped my way past the dozens of pleasure cruisers, yachts, and the boatyard. I knew a few of the workers and waved as I went by.

I got to a sign which advertised diving lessons, sea fishing and short coastal trips. Looking towards the water, I saw the boat owned and run by the Northerners, the trio of semi-psychotic ex-football hooligans who, for a fee, had been such a help rescuing in Isabella Cabrera. They were great, if boisterous, drinking companions.

Yorkie emerged from below deck with a can of varnish in one hand and a brush in the other. Divested of his Leeds United shirt, he was definitely fat, but it was the kind of fat that covered huge muscularity formed on the building sites of West Yorkshire, topped out by regular bouts of Powerlifting and mindless violence.

'Eyup, Danny, where you off to, then?'

'Just a bit of a walk and a beer. What's happening with you?'

'The Mancs are finishing a tiling job off in an apartment and I'm just tarting t'boat up a bit.'

'The Mancs' were the other two of the trio, Manchester City supporters who, despite the recent successes of their beloved team and its clearly better record, indulged and tolerated the bizarre affiliation of their companion with a mixture of condescension and pity.

'I'll see you on the way back.'

He waved and carried on varnishing; the brush tiny in his ham fist.

I took the lift to the terrace and got a beer. The place was about a quarter full and I got a seat looking out across the Marina and towards my villa.

My phone rang. It was Uzcudzen.

'Danny, I have some interesting info for you.'

'I hope I'm not causing any problems by asking you, Paulino.'

'Under normal circumstances, I would not be able to do this, Danny, but you may be onto something that interests me.'

I was not prepared to damage my relationship with Uzcudzen. He could have easily put me away for a good few years, and still could. He had shown that his adherence to the law and the usual protocols of law enforcement was creative to say the least. He wasn't going to expose himself to criticism for something as basic as a car registration check, but I knew that if something really serious came up, he was not above making the evidence fit the crime.

'The car owner and the description you gave leads me to believe that the man is Lorenzo Vitria, a man who years ago was of great interest to the Police in mainland Spain. He has convictions for illegal gambling, and set up a major national network of unlawful bookmakers when he was in his early twenties. By the time he was thirty, he was untouchable. He set himself brilliantly up behind a number of stooges, corporations and expensive lawyers.'

'Well, that's interesting,' I said. Vitria sounded dangerous.

'Vitria made a lot of money, then he had what can only be called an epiphany. It appears his brother was an addicted gambler who lost everything – his home, marriage, and family, and in despair killed himself. Lorenzo knew nothing of his brother's issues, nonetheless, his family ostracized him.'

A criminal with a conscience? I wondered how Vitria had got involved with Jessica. Uzcudzen continued.

'One day, he walked into the Prosecutors office in Madrid, asked to see an investigator and told them everything. He handed over several million in the following weeks. He was so open, the tax authorities judged that he was actually entitled to retain some of his wealth.'

'That's some turnaround,' I said.

'He went on to advise the government in drawing up the Spanish Gambling Act, which was a world leader in predicting the growth in online gambling. He's made a second fortune acting as a consultant to governments all over the world on gambling legislation – also by some very early and prudent investments in entirely legal online gambling.'

'I'm not sure what I expected, Paulino, but not that. So, he's a good guy?'

'Danny, I have no reason to believe that he's anything other than a model citizen. He has very powerful contacts with the Spanish government who regard his advisory services to other governments as being very good for Spain's reputation. Whatever you're up to, proceed with caution with this guy.'

'Is he married? What's his domestic situation?'

'No marriage recorded. He lives near La Laguna – a very nice house, no heavy-duty security, just alarms and some CCTV. Local cops say they have never had a call to the house – no known or perceived threats. He eats in a couple of local top-end restaurants, usually alone. He supports local charities. In all – low key, *buena ciudadano.*'

'What about the girls?'

'Nothing yet, Danny. There's nothing on the Spanish system, as the ladies come from the Caribbean. I've put out a couple of enquiries, low key, avoiding the major information systems, but it looks as though we've never had contact with them.'

I thanked Uzcudzen and hung up. I walked back to the village, acknowledged Yorkie and the guys in the boatyard and went to my car. It was time for a trip to La Laguna.

Chapter Thirteen

San Cristobal de la Laguna, better known simply as La Laguna, is the second largest city in Tenerife and sits alongside the largest, Santa Cruz, joined by a tram system. It is the cultural heart of the Canary Islands and its original capital.

Centuries ago, it was the home of the infamous corsair and pirate Amaro Pargo, a man who made a fortune from illegal activities but became a major benefactor to the poor and an invaluable servant to his country. Perhaps a forerunner of the man I was investigating, Lorenzo Vitria.

***

Vitria's villa was on the outskirts in the foothills of Mount Teide, the huge volcano that dominates the Island no matter which part of it you are on. Protected by a high wall and electronically activated gates, the villa gave the impression of being secluded rather than a fortress. Mature Bougainvillea showed its pink flowers over the top of the wall.

I parked about half a mile away, on the rise of the mountain. I mounted a tripod and placed my camera on it to give the impression to passing drivers of a keen photographer taking pictures of the magnificent mountain. In fact, from this position, facing away from the mountain and using my military-strength binoculars, I had a good view into the garden and grounds of the villa.

The garden and pool area were surrounded by the walls, the front set back some hundred yards from the road. At the rear, there was a vineyard and olive grove. Abutting the walls were dense, well-grown bushes.

I saw a black woman lounging under an umbrella – it was Jessica. She wore skimpy bikini bottoms. After a while, Vitria came out with a tray of drinks and sat with her. They talked and I got the impression that Vitria was doing most of the talking. I saw Jessica take out a tissue – she appeared to be wiping away tears. She wasn't imprisoned, and Vitria seemed caring and concerned.

I decided to return to El Nautico and tell Emilie face-to-face what I had found. I texted her to let her know I was on my way.

As I drove back, I tried to rationalize what was going on. By the time I got to Emilie's apartment, things were no clearer. I got to the car park and checked my phone. She hadn't replied. Entering the reception, the phone went. It was Emilie. I told her I was there, and she told me she would tell the security guard to allow me to come down to the swimming pool.

Emilie was, like her sister earlier, sitting under an umbrella. She was wearing a micro bikini that left very little to the imagination.

Unlike the shy, embarrassed woman I had first encountered at the Duck, she was now on her own territory. Very comfortable in her near nudity, she stood and pulled out a chair to allow me to set down my stick and rest my always aching knees. She sat beside me.

'What have you learned, Danny?'

'Jessica is safe. She is living with a man called Vitria. He's a wealthy man who lives near La Laguna. I am yet to find out quite what their relationship is, but she seems to be in no danger.'

Emilie was clearly impressed.

'Thank you, Danny – that's more information than I thought possible. You're a good detective.' A bead of sweat ran down her chest into her cleavage. I thought she would melt. 'Have you eaten, Danny?'

I followed her into her apartment. Emilie made a plate of olives, cooked meats and a little cheese. she passed me a bottle of Cava and pointed out the ice machine. I opened the wine and put it in an ice-filled bucket.

We sat on her balcony looking out towards the west. The sun was going down, the food was good, the wine cold and refreshing. She went for a shower. At her invitation, I joined her.

At that moment, Tina Turner was singing 'What's Love Got to Do with It?' in my headphones. *Probably nothing, Tina, but I'll take this for the time being.*

***

The sun rose over the red rock that separates El Medano from the rest of the southern stretch of the coast. I rose and dressed.

During the night, Emilie had told me things about Jessica that disturbed me. She was a talented musician but had always been troubled. Highly intelligent, she had qualified to go to University in France and while there, had dabbled in extreme politics. On her return to Guadeloupe, she had secretly joined the Revolutionary Armed Organization, a small but violent group of extreme left-wing activists. They had been quickly infiltrated and betrayed and Jessica had been lucky to only serve a short time in prison.

On her release, she returned to France and Emilie had followed her to try to ensure she kept out of trouble. All had seemed well but some months ago, she started behaving oddly. She had worked on a tour with a classical orchestra in Germany and France. Emilie had been working on a cruise at the same time. Their return to Tenerife coincided and they spent about a week together. During this time, Jessica had received several phone calls and she had become highly secretive about them.

Jessica's conversations with her sister had been about how the rich got their money, what filth they were, and how she would kill someone with money with no remorse.

Then they had gone their own way for a few months, planning to be together now. In their telephone conversations, Jessica hadn't recanted one bit. She had told Emilie that once on the concert platform, she had imagined toting a high-powered machine gun and riddling the audience. She was clearly a lady with issues.

My concern was that she was now with a wealthy man, in his villa, alone. I phoned Uzcudzen.

'I've had no response, Danny. I'm waiting for the Caribbean guys to talk to the French guys who will in turn speak to me. As soon as I know something, I'll get back to you.' In retrospect, I should have opened up to Paulino Uzcudzen there and then, but I didn't.

I'd learned as a cop that if you couldn't detect and arrest, you should prevent and save. I decided to drive back to La Laguna to confront Jessica and Vitria. I would probably get thrown out. Vitria was no angel – he may have been out of circulation for a long time, but the life he had matured in was tough; he would know how to look after himself. In Jessica, I could be dealing with either a trained terrorist or a lunatic, maybe both.

I arrived at the villa. It was 10am. I had left Emilie sleeping, hoping to have a resolution for her on my return. I parked and walked to the main gate where I activated the intercom. A male voice asked who I was. I told him I needed to speak to Senor Vitria urgently. In my ears, Sinatra was singing 'Someone to Watch Over Me'. *Good idea, Frank.*

Vitria opened the gate and met me at the villa door. He looked bemused at the sight of this crippled man hobbling towards him. I asked if we could talk privately. He walked me to the pool and solemnly bade me to sit.

I ran through the story: of how Emilie had hired me, how I had found him and Jessica, what I knew about Jessica and her terrorist affiliations and hatred of certain sections of society. That, based on what I had learned, I thought he may be in danger.

'Mr Mclinden, you have this wrong.' He was about to put his side of the story when my phone rang. It was Emilie. I excused myself.

'Danny, where are you?'

'I'm in La Laguna.'

'Are you with Jessica and the boyfriend?' I could hear traffic: she was driving.

'Yes, let me get back to you.' I hung up.

I turned back to Vitria. I hadn't heard her approach but standing behind him was Jessica. Vitria took her hand as she sat at the table. She eyed me suspiciously.

'Mr Mclinden, tell Jessica what you told me,' Vitria said.

I looked her straight in the eye and told her. She started to weep. I hadn't expected this reaction.

Vitria spoke. 'As I was saying, you have this wrong.'

Another interruption: I heard a car pull up on the pebbled drive and the sound of a car door closing. The intercom beeper sounded.

'Excuse me, I'll just see who this is,' said Vitria. He was holding Jessica's hand. He let it go and patted her shoulder. She continued to cry. Vitria walked towards the gate. My phone rang. It was Uzcudzen.

'I've got the info, Danny. There are two sisters – Jessica and Emilie. Jessica is a top-class musician, a cellist, plays with leading orchestras all over the world. Her sister Emilie is a nightmare, spent time in the loony bin in France – besotted with her sister, hates her success, tried to kill her in Biarritz a year ago.'

I started to get to my feet. My knees hurt. I tried to shout at Vitria, who was about ten metres from the gate.

Uzcudzen was still talking.

'She's got definite terrorist connections, will know how to use a gun, was suspected to be involved in a bomb attack on a market in Dresden – the Germans couldn't prove it.'

I was stumbling after Vitria. My voice wouldn't come. I struck out with my stick and hit some gardening tools, making them fall just to make a noise. As Vitria opened the gate, he heard the noise and hesitated. I saw the gun, a 22, deadly close up.

I was alongside Vitria. I pushed him aside. The gun went off as I brought the heavy stick down on Emile's head.

***

I awoke in the hospital in Santa Cruz. The first sensation was pain, but that was an old friend. The second sensation was the tinnitus. It wasn't gone, although it seemed easier – the pain was in my head. I looked around and sitting next the bed was Uzcudzen. Next to him were Vitria and Jessica.

'Hello Danny,' Uzcudzen said. There were smiles all round.

'What happened, Paulino?'

'You got shot, amigo.'

'Where?'

'In the place it would do least harm, your head.'

'Emilie?'

'In custody – in hospital care, also with a very sore head.'

'I didn't mean to hit her that hard.'

'You did her a favour. Maybe now she can get some treatment – at least she's no longer a danger.'

I looked at Jessica.

'Are you OK?' I asked.

She smiled, and we all talked for a while. Jessica was both concerned and relieved about her sister. Clearly Emilie had been a nightmare for years. The story about her working on cruise ships as a singer and being a recording artist were all lies.

Jessica had met Vitria after a concert in Vienna, shortly after Emilie had attacked her. They had Tenerife in common and arranged to meet there. When they did meet up, Jessica's situation with Emilie was still at an all-time low and knowing Emilie was about to return to the island, she took off with Vitria.

I was still bemused.

'How did she know where we were, where the villa was?'

Uzcudzen smiled.

'I assume you spent the night with her, my friend? While you were asleep, she activated the tracker on your phone. It was turned on at three am.'

I touched the dressing on the small hole in my skull. The bullet had travelled through and upward, leaving the brain untouched; another scar to add to my mounting collection.

Also, I have added a collection of music for the cello to my music library, given to me by two new friends.

Chapter Fourteen

Golf del Sur is a short drive from Reina Sofia airport, or as it's better known to English speakers, Tenerife South airport. Most visitors arriving for the first time use the excellent taxi service that can whisk them the short distance to the Golf or the hour or so to Los Gigantes or any of the myriad other destinations to be visited and enjoyed in between.

It was from one of these taxis that three people emerged one day in the Golf: Mr and Mrs Rabbits and Mr Howard.

I was sitting on the terrace of the Duck enjoying a lunchtime Corona when they arrived. In my ears, keeping the Tinnitus at bay, the Percy Faith orchestra were playing 'Delicado'. It's a great tune to have in the background while you're people-watching.

The newcomers gathered their luggage from the taxi and the older of the men, Mr Rabbits, paid the driver. They went into the reception of the 5-star hotel next the Edificio I had lived in when I first arrived in the Golf, near the office I shared with my friend and business partner Guillermo Cabrera.

A few minutes later, they emerged sans luggage and made their way, as do so many new arrivals, to the welcoming portal of the Tame Duck.

All was not well. Mrs Rabbits was not amused. The two men took a seat outside, next to my table.

Mrs Rabbits entered the bar looking for the lady's conveniences, her capacious behind swaying as she entered, emitting belligerence.

'Hi,' I greeted the two men.

'Hi,' answered the friendly young man I would come to know as Ian Howard.

'Good afternoon,' answered the downtrodden misery I would come to know as Bernard (Bunny) Rabbits.

'Is everything OK?'

Ian looked at Bunny sympathetically.

'We've arrived a little early and our rooms aren't ready for an hour.'

'Don't worry, they're very good. If they say an hour, they mean it, and the rooms are really good.'

'I'm afraid my wife takes such things very personally – she's very difficult to please,' said Bunny.

Anne, one of the barmaids who doubled up as waitress during the day, came over and asked if they would like a drink. They looked at my beer and ordered two for themselves. Anne walked back inside the bar, almost colliding with Mrs Rabbits as she exited.

'Filthy.'

'What is, dear?' asked Bunny.

'The facilities – horrible.'

Now I understood. I knew she was a plonker – one thing you could always say about the Duck under the management of Ronnie and Wendy was that the dunnies were spotless.

For the next thirty minutes, while drinking water, Mrs Rabbits regaled her husband with all the wrongs he had committed during their twenty-five years together: his career failures, her sacrifices, and this horrible place he had made her come to.

I gathered that Ian and Bunny worked together. It sounded as though it was something to do with finance and I found out later that they were accountants.

They had been working on some project to do with a huge construction site where the subcontractors, about a thousand in all, had all been netted by the taxman.

They set up a committee to fight this apparently unfair imposition and Bunny, hearing of the problem, had offered to represent them, also organising solicitors from his numerous contacts. His offer had brought his firm over a thousand new clients and had created some very hard work for himself and Ian, but with Ian's help, had ended up with the taxman at bay, some very happy customers and a delighted employer.

Recognizing Bunny's contribution, his employers had treated him and his wife, plus Ian, to a week away in Tenerife at a nice five-star hotel.

Holidays had never featured heavily in the lives of the Rabbits. For the first ten years of their marriage, they had gone to stay in a caravan on the Yorkshire coast with her sister and mother. When the termagant that was his mother-in-law had the great courtesy to slip off the mortal coil and go and sing out of tune in the eternal choir, he had raised the prospect of travelling abroad.

'What about our Moira?' was the standard answer. 'Our Moira' being the spinster sister: soft of brain, hard of heart, with the face of a Rottweiler chewing a bee and a disposition to match. The thought of 'our Moira' being left alone or a holiday in anything other than a cramped caravan under the leaden Yorkshire skies was anathema to June Rabbits.

Bunny managed to convince his wife that his employers wouldn't look kindly on him if he turned down the award of the week's holiday in Tenerife. The accountancy firm had included June in the holiday, so she should come. Bunny sorted out the passports, and here they were.

Everything about Tenerife irritated June Rabbits: it was too hot; too windy. There were too many foreigners, too many Brits, the food was poor, the water tasted funny. The only thing she looked forward to was sitting in their room watching *Eastenders*, and subsequent meandering telephone conversations with her sister. During *Eastenders*, Bunny managed to slip away and join Ian in the Duck.

Ian had quickly separated himself from the Rabbits. Immediately, he realised that any attempts at establishing a friendship with June were a complete waste of time. He spent time around the pool and was getting on rather well with a group of people his own age.

He phoned Bunny to see how he was getting along, and in sympathy, arranged to meet him at the Duck in the early evening while the battle-axe was distracted by the events in Walford.

'Bunny, why do you stand for it?' asked Ian, his normal circumspection retarded by an earlier intake of Sangria with his new friends, being topped up by a couple of Corona 4.5%.

'I'm just used to it, Ian,' came the lame reply. He was rarely challenged by anyone about his apparent acceptance of his wife's behaviour. On this occasion, it caused him to reflect on the twenty-five years he had endured with her.

Their physical relationship had ended within a few years of their marriage: a marriage that in retrospect he realised had been arranged between his mother, June's mother, and June herself.

He cursed his weak will, trapped in a loveless marriage with a woman he had realised long ago that he hated.

'I think you deserve a bloody medal – I'll get us another.'

'No, Ian, I have to get back to the room.'

'Why?'

Before Bunny answered, he considered what his natural response was going to be. He was going to say 'because *Eastenders* will be ending'.

He actually said: 'Go on then, and I'll have another Corona and one of those, what do you call them? Chasers?'

The tequila hit the back of his throat and caused a prickling sensation through his body. He calmed this by a long pull on the Corona.

Meanwhile, Ian had struck up a conversation with three Northerners who had followed them into the bar, all wearing football shirts, with aggressively short hair and tattoos. Not the type of chap you met at the Rotary club, but they were funny.

The largest was just that: large – massive shoulders, framing an equally massive chest and a large belly. The 5xl Leeds United shirt was pulled tight across his frame. He downed pints of beer as though he was putting out a fire.

'Na then, me owd pal, whats thi name? I'm Matt – call me Yorky.'

'I'm Bernard – call me Bunny.'

The quiet, thin, balding, persecuted accountant was soon forming a friendship with the huge, loud, hairy builder/diver/ex-football hooligan.

The night wore on. At 9.30pm, the music started promptly. Ronnie introduced the star guest at 10pm. Tonight, it was the "famous" Belinda Wheeler, a white-blonde lady who did a Tina Turner tribute act which included songs from the Supremes, Martha Vandella, Aretha Franklyn and many other artists – all black singers. In fact, the only thing about Belinda's act that was not black was Belinda herself.

Soon, the place was packed. Groups of unattended women were dancing around their handbags, and the booze was flowing.

Taking a break from their discourse on the contribution of hooliganism to football history and the benefits of Rotary club membership, Yorkie and Bunny and their male companions observed the gyrations on the dance floor. Bunny was having a serious wobble, the tequila doing its job.

Nonetheless, when a rather voluptuous lady with a magnificent cleavage approached him, took him by the hand and led him to the dance floor, the applause and support from Ian, Yorkie and the male-dominated bar area instilled him with a confidence he had not experienced, other than when he was presented with a set of figures no one else could fathom.

Belinda was singing 'Steamy Windows,' a song that necessitates, while holding the lady in the standard ballroom hold, as befits a Rotary club member, a gyratory series of movements by both parties that, under the right circumstances, can inspire both eroticism and non-medical priapism. Bunny was doing very well for a novice, to cheers from his new gang of friends.

It was inevitable that at this point, his humourless, bad-hearted bitch of a wife made her appearance. June Rabbits marched across the dancefloor, taking hold of Bunny, and dragged him to the door. Her face was red and clearly furious. It wouldn't have been surprising if steam had been emanating from both ears.

Howls of derision were aimed at June, to no avail. Bunny was drunk but terrified. He showed no resistance, cowering under the onslaught of the whey-faced old nag that had once been a woman he'd tried to love.

She marched him back the hotel, through the reception and into the lift. As she dragged him along, she berated him.

'I'll show you…How dare you…What a showing up…I never wanted to come here…'

Other guests displayed a mixture of alarm and amusement at the plight of the little man with the monstrous wife.

Their room was on the third floor. How June Rabbits came to fall from her apartment balcony into the pool remains a mystery, save to say that she hit the water head-first and although it broke her fall, her misfortune was that she landed in the shallow end and caused a serious injury to her neck.

When the hotel staff and a wobbly Bunny ran to her aid, they found her in what can only be described as a black apoplexy: her baleful eyes expressing unspeakable abuse.

Bunny phoned Ian who came back to the hotel immediately and accompanied the couple as an ambulance conveyed them to the nearest A&E department.

The ambulance carried her slowly and carefully to the hospital. Bunny held her hand solicitously and sought to comfort her, after all, they had been married for a quarter of a century. Despite this, her bitterness and bad nature showed through. Her determination to cause misery and dominate Bunny was unrelenting. Ian sat silently, taking in the sad scene and mentally recording June's unrelenting anger.

'If I die and you see another woman, I'll crawl from my coffin and haunt you.'

Those were her last words.

Bunny sat and looked at the body and mourned. On arrival at the hospital, June was pronounced dead and taken to the mortuary.

***

I was in the small, quiet back bar in the Duck later that night when Yorkie spotted me. I was aware that there had been some hilarity earlier regarding a wife catching her husband having a quick gallivant.

'Ey up, cock.' He seemed rather subdued.

'What's happening, Yorkie?'

'Tha knows that lad that's staying in five-star wi' 'is missis and a mate?'

I remembered Bunny and Ian and the unforgettable June.

'Yes, they must be due to go back to UK soon.'

'She's dead – fell off balcony intut pool.'

'when?' My eyes widened in shock.

'Just na. Ian – the younger lad, phoned me from t'ospital. Cops have got Bunny. Ian sez he needs a lawyer. Weers Cabrera?'

I phoned Guillermo. He arranged for a local criminal lawyer to attend the Police Station.

Within a couple of hours, Bunny was released, on the proviso that he wouldn't leave the island until the investigations were completed.

The case was passed to the Guardia Civil and after a couple of days, Bunny was re interviewed by detectives and a date set for the Coroners court. In the meantime, Bunny took a leave of absence from his London office. Ian had also stayed over but was due to return to work.

The day Ian flew back to Gatwick, we met him for a farewell drink: the Northerners, Ronnie, Cabrera, Bunny and me. We sat on the terrace outside the Duck.

Bunny announced that, pending the result of the Coroner's enquiry, he intended to have June buried in Tenerife. He also revealed that after consultation with the Northerners, they had invited him to join them in their business enterprises. They needed better organization, and financial and quality control. He also fancied learning how to captain a day cruise boat and maybe learning how to dive. He would not, therefore, be returning to the UK.

As they left, all the guys shook hands with Ian. He was left with just Bunny and me. Ian picked up his suitcase as the taxi taking him to the airport pulled up.

'Bunny – I have to ask you – June's last words chilled me to the bone – when she said that if you took up with another woman, she would crawl out of her grave and haunt you. That must be on your mind.'

'I've thought about that, Ian. That's why I want to have her buried here. I've told the undertaker – I want her interred face down, so when she starts digging, she's got a long way to go.'

Chapter Fifteen

In the Golf, not many men wear ties. Casually sloppy if you're holiday or are one of the many retirees, casually smart if you're on business. This is the norm.

The visitor to my office was wearing a tie that was as bright as the sunset. His hair was short, black, and greying; his cheeks pinched and florid either with too much sun or blood pressure; his nose showing the blue early stages of a "gin bloom". His clothes fitted him in a loose insouciance; his small pink ears clashed with his tie but otherwise fitted well in the kaleidoscope of colour that was his face.

He sat by my desk, leaning forward as I rested one elbow on the desk. My hand was on the African Hardwood cane that had become my trademark.

'I want you to find what happened to him. I hope you never actually find him.' His green eyes stared solemnly at me.

I rocked back in the chair. His face, given an almost demonic cast by the shape of his chin, mouth, nose, and thin eyebrows, was as interesting as his voice.

'Why?'

'I've been told you're a man I can confide in, Danny. May I call you Danny?'

I smiled, I nodded. He was going to spend money; it was the least I could do.

'And any fair price is good enough for your services.'

My smile broadened.

'That's fine, but I've got to know what you want of me. I understand you're interested in a Russian, Sergei Valuev. You want to know what's happened to him but aren't bothered what that is?'

The man in the loud tie lowered his voice conspiratorially.

'In a certain way I do. For instance, if you did happen to find him and could arrange for him to stay away from Tenerife for good, that would be worth a lot of money to me.'

'You mean even if he didn't want to stay away?'

'Correct.'

I continued smiling but shook my head.

'I doubt you've got the kind of money I would consider for the particular service you would like.'

He looked a little disappointed but continued staring at me.

'Well, tell me the story, Mr Corker. You don't mind if I call you Arthur, do you?' I asked.

'Valuev has a girlfriend. I like her. They had an almighty row last week and he took off. If she thinks he's gone for good, there's a chance I could move in on her.'

'I'd need to speak to her, Arthur. Who is Valuev? What does he do?'

'He is a ponce, doesn't do anything worthwhile – artist, karaoke clown – a bum.'

'Can you tell me anything about him that might indicate where he may be?'

'It might be better if you talk to his woman, Natalia.'

***

A large woman opened the apartment door. Her red, loose-fitting, strapless dress was offset by a heavy silver necklace. She was full-bosomed and shapely, with a self confidence that could be called arrogance in one less graceful.

'Natalia?'

She hesitated. I always made sure I stood well back when I was meeting women in a confined space. I knew the sight of me was disconcerting: the limp, the unusual frozen look of my face.

'Yes, can I help you?' She was possibly Russian, certainly East European.

'Arthur Corker sent me to see you. My name is Danny Mclinden – I'm a private detective. He asked me to find your friend, the Russian.'

She relaxed. 'Have you found him?'

'I need to talk to you first.' I produced a business card: Mclinden and Cabrera, Sunset Investigations.

'OK, please come in.' She stepped back, pulling the door open. She led me to the balcony, which overlooked the sea, and asked me to sit down.

'Did Arthur tell you why he wanted to find Sergei?'

'Yes, he thinks that if Sergei is gone for good, he may have a chance with you.'

She smiled but gave nothing away. I expected her to show shock or surprise at my candour; she showed me nothing.

'Has he left like this before?'

'All the time.'

'What kind of man is he?'

'He's a good man, when he's sober. Even when he's drunk or high, he's OK, except with women and cash.'

'That leaves a lot of scope. What does he do for a living?'

'Elvis act – in Russian. He also plays poker.'

'Nobody makes a good living that way.'

'He comes up with a little cash now and then.' She smiled, rather ironically.

'How long have you been with him?'

'Two years.'

'Always in Tenerife?'

'Yes.'

'He's Russian?'

'Muscovite.'

'Where are you from?'

'You're not looking for me, Danny.' She folded her arms and I sensed that I had overstepped the mark.

'Does he have many friends?'

She laughed sardonically. 'Friends, there's a concept…'

'He must know people?'

'There's a guy called Spinoza. There's Yuri and a man he calls Ray.'

'Who are they?'

'Just men he knows, all low-lifes. I don't know anything about them, they just phone or call here to pick him up.'

'Do you think they'll know where he is?'

'No, they keep phoning to see if he's turned up.'

'Any other women?'

She frowned. 'There's a couple but I have no idea of names.'

'Did he have any money when he left?'

'He had about fifty euros, no cards.'

'Did he say anything before he left?'

'Just that with a bit of luck he would be back that evening with a present for me.'

'Were you getting along together OK?'

'Yes, we had a falling out a couple of days before, but we patched it up.'

'Any photos of him?'

She passed me a photograph of a good-looking man, dark hair, sideburns. Definitely a touch of Elvis.

I stood to leave, and she followed me towards the door.

'Is his act any good?'

'If it's a Russian audience, not bad at all – trouble is, there aren't that many Russian-only places. He has an agent.' She passed me a card with his agent's details. Lawrie Binnet, a Brit if the name was anything to go by, certainly an Anglo.

'If you think of anything, please give me a call.' I pointed to the business card in her hand.

I phoned Ronnie. I asked him about the Russian Elvis. He had seen him a few times when he first came to the island. He dressed in Elvis's white Vegas jumpsuit; did all the moves, including the karate kicks. Trouble was, he sang *Hotel California*, which was as far from being an Elvis song as you could get. Ronnie said it was the funniest thing he had seen in years, made even funnier by the Russian's complete seriousness.

Ronnie told me that he'd heard that Sergei's agent, Lawrie Binnet, was not a good guy. He was into a few things besides being an artists' agent. He was known to rip off acts. Ronnie would never use him.

I went to Binnet's office. It was situated in a business centre in the middle of Los Christianos' commercial district. It wasn't what I expected. The furnishings were very tasteful, and there was a smart, attractive, and very professional receptionist.

I told her I was a bar owner, seeking to set up a regular supply of good quality acts. She went into an adjoining office and returned a few minutes later, informing me that Binnet was with someone but would only be a short while.

She offered me coffee. I declined. She smiled in the way good receptionists do with prospective clients. Minutes passed.

A shot rang out and a woman screamed on the other side of the double doors. I got to my feet and hobbled to the doors, reaching them at the same time as the receptionist. We opened a door each and went through, the noise from the gun still reverberating from the walls and ceilings.

I got in front of the receptionist and shielded her as we entered Binnet's office. Behind the desk, the man I correctly assumed to be Lawrie Binnet had a small, bloody hole in his forehead. Blood and grey matter coated a section of the blinds and the glass on the window behind him. He was definitely dead.

There was another door leading from Binnet's office. It was open. Lying in the service corridor it led to was the unconscious body of a woman. She was face down, breathing but badly whacked on the head. Blood ran from her scalp into her forehead, clearly showing where she had been hit. I heard someone running down the stairs, leading to an alternative exit.

I placed her in the recovery position. People were coming into the room from other offices in the complex: excited, confused, and alarmed. The receptionist asked for someone to call the police and an ambulance.

A guy bent down to assist me with the injured woman and took.

I took the chance to find the route the shooter must have used. I limped down the stairs as fast as I could. Even though I can only manage one step at a time, I am not much slower than the average person in an emergency.

One floor down, there was a door that led into the busy street. It was an emergency exit but the crash bar had been used and the door stood open.

I reached the door and looked out onto a typical Los Christianos working day; the sun-baked streets quiet. There was a lottery ticket booth opposite the doorway, and a café next door to the business centre. I decided to ask if anyone had seen anything.

***

By the time I got back upstairs, I could hear the sirens. I watched as an office worker from a neighbouring business administered first aid to the unconscious woman. Then the pain in my legs kicked in and I sat in the reception area.

I had already noticed the magazines advertising top-end luxury goods and services populating the coffee table. An aquarium with an array of colourful tiny tropical fish graced one corner. Binnet had money, or at least he used to have money before someone blew his brains out.

Soon I was being grilled by two of Tenerife's finest uniformed officers of the Guardia Civil. I told them who I was, what had happened, and what I was doing there. The questioning stopped while phone calls were made about me.

Thirty minutes later, the main door opened. In walked Colonel Paulino Uzcudzen, accompanied by his aides; two immaculate younger men who reeked of university, fast promotion, and ambition. They stood either side of the door.

Uzcudzen, a man who still held my fate in his hands, sat opposite me, calm, immaculate, in charge.

'Hi Danny,' he said. He didn't seem surprised to find me at a crime scene.

'Paulino.'

'What happened?'

I told him. 'Then I went into the street, looked around but couldn't see anything. I went into the café next door – but no one had noticed anyone leave by the emergency exit, and the lottery ticket seller's blind. But you might pick something up on CCTV.'

'We're already looking. What do you know about the dead guy?'

I recounted Ronnie's opinion of Lawrie Binnet. I also said that I'd expected to meet a dead-beat, in a dead-beat office, not this expensive, plush luxury.

'What about the woman?'

'No idea, but the receptionist must know.'

'She's in shock – they've taken her to hospital – bad asthma reaction – but we'll talk to her later.'

'Can I go?'

'Certainly, amigo. I know where I can find you.'

Uzcudzen was always friendly. Like a tame tiger when it's been fed, he lets you tickle his tummy. But remember to keep feeding him. If you don't, he becomes extremely dangerous.

I stumped out of the office, my cane tapping on the expensive marble floor. My knees were hurting after the hasty trip to the emergency exit and the act of kneeling beside the injured woman. I popped a painkiller and took the lift to the ground floor.

I drove back to Natalia's apartment. It was virtually on the ground floor, up a few steps, facing the street. Well-kept window boxes adorned the windows. I knocked. The door was open. Natalia stood in the hallway; two suitcases packed, standing alongside her. Clearly, she was waiting to be collected.

'Where are you going?'

'It's nothing to do with you. I've had enough. I'm getting out.'

'Lawrie Binnet is dead.'

The shock hit her hard. She sat down suddenly.

'Jesus Christ.'

'A woman has been badly hurt at his office as well.'

'Christina?'

'Who's she?'

'She's his secretary – works in the reception.'

'No, she's OK. It's another woman – older, a redhead.'

Natalia's face gave away nothing, but I heard a movement at the rear of the apartment.

'Who's here, Natalia?'

Before she answered, a door opened, and it was immediately clear. Elvis had not left the building.

Sergei Valuev's resemblance to the King was striking, enhanced by hair dyed jet-black, and sideburns. His appearance was let down by his unkempt stubble and scruffy clothes. He was holding a long-bladed butcher's knife.

I told him to put it down. Natalia told him to put it down. He looked unsure, so I whacked his wrist with my heavy cane and he dropped it.

'If you bend down to pick it up, you will stay down. I'm not here to hurt you, but I will.'

Valuev slumped into an armchair and I retrieved the knife. He was defeated, by me, by life.

'Sergei – one man is definitely dead, a woman is teetering on the edge of death in the ICU and no one knows what the fuck is going on. Other than me, and all I know is that you're involved in some way.'

Natalia spoke to him. 'Did you kill Binnet?'

'Binnet is dead?' he said, looking at me.

'Shot in the head, dead centre,' I told him.

His reaction mirrored Natalia's.

'Are you going to tell me what's going on or do I just call the cops?'

'Binnet is…was…a trafficker in girls. I owed him gambling money, a lot of money. He had his guys beat me up a couple of times, then he threatened to hurt Natalia.' Valuev looked at her as he spoke. 'I'm so sorry.'

This was obviously news to Natalia, who hung on to his every word.

'He made me go with the other three guys to Santa Cruz to pick up a new consignment of girls from Eastern Europe from the ferry. They had been recruited to work in the hotels and restaurants – actually, they were headed for sex work. He has a finca – a farm – up the mountain, very remote. We took them there. Then in shifts, we made sure they were kept under control, until they were scared enough to do as they were told. It was horrible, but the other three guys are evil bastards, and

I was terrified they would harm Natalia unless I helped them and paid my debts off.'

'How many girls?'

'Seven. We expected about ten, but seven were easier to handle.'

'Where are they now?'

'Still there. I left them with the three other guys and the woman.'

'What woman?'

'Trixie. She's Binnet's number one. The guys are evil but she's satanic.'

'What does she look like?'

'Short, stocky, redhead.'

She sounded like the lady from Binnet's office, the one with the bad headache.

'Tell me about the girls.'

'Three are Romanian – very lovely, dark like gypsy. Two are Polska – blonde girls – also beautiful. Trixie say she will get a lot of money for them from North Africans. Two others are Russian. I talk to them a lot – intelligent, nice girls. Student is one – the other was going to join army like her brother. Just came to Tenerife for a year to earn cash, look around.'

'Why haven't you tried to help them? Natalia asked.

'I was scared about you,' he said, shamefaced.

'Bullshit – you were scared about yourself.'

'I did try to help one girl. I let her send a message to her brother, saying she's OK.'

'How?' I asked.

'By text.'

Chapter Sixteen

The Yasanevo district of Moscow houses many administrative buildings, schools, and high-end offices. It's also home to the HQ of the Foreign Intelligence Service of the Russian Federation.

As part of their training, a group of suitable young Russian army officers are seconded to FISRF for a period in order to better understand the threats to Mother Russia and the methods by which the homeland is protected.

One of these, Captain Leonid Barashovsky, was working his way through the various departments when his mother contacted him, informing him that she was worried about his younger sister, Irana. She had travelled to the paradise island of Tenerife to start a job in a hotel, but she hadn't been in touch for a week.

Leonid tried to phone Irana, but her phone battery must be flat or otherwise out of action. He contacted the Russian consul in Santa Cruz, but they were unable to help, other than to confirm that Irana had arrived on the ferry from Cadiz some days earlier. Leonid then contacted the Guardia Civil in Tenerife, who placed Irana on their missing persons list.

Mrs Barashovsky, a widow of a former high-ranking military man, was frantic. Leonid was about to request a leave of absence to go to Tenerife, when two messages arrived on his phone from an unfamiliar number.

The first message read: *Hi, everything is OK. My own phone is broken. I will be in touch soon.*

The second message said: *Help us! Lia and me are imprisoned with five other girls. I'm in deep trouble. There are seven of us.*

Leonid walked straight into the office of the highest-ranking comms specialist. He explained that his sister was missing and showed him the messages. He explained that he believed her to be in Tenerife. Without a word, the senior officer went into a busy adjoining Control Room. In fifteen minutes, he was back.

'The message came from a farmhouse on a mountainside in Tenerife.'

'What can we do?'

'Russian citizens seem to be being held against their will. The Spaniards are slow and indecisive – we will send people.'

Leonid returned to the apartment supplied to him during his attachment. He phoned his mother and told her not to worry; that the situation was coming under control. He waited. He couldn't sleep. At midnight, there was a knock at his door. Two men stood there, in civilian clothes, fit, hard-eyed. These were the men who were going to help Irana, and he was going with them.

***

The Russian consul in Santa Cruz was irritated by the timing of the call from Moscow, but he soon remembered his place when he realised the status of the high official who had called him.

He was, by any means possible, to find out who owned a particular Finca situated in a remote area in the south of the island. This had to be done by midday.

A visit to the local town hall, a flash of his credentials and a fifty euro note, and he had the information that it was owned by an English entertainment agent called Lawrie Binnet with an office in Los Christianos. By 1030 hours, a phone call to Moscow ended the consul's involvement.

The Spanish Town Hall clerk had seen the previous evening's news, about an Englishman murdered in Los Christianos, with a woman also badly injured. He shrugged his shoulders, pocketed the fifty Euros, and, following protocol, phoned the Guardia Civil to tell them the Russian Consul had just called.

***

Uzcudzen received an email informing him that the Russians were interested in a property owned by the murdered Brit. He read it, thought for moment, finished his coffee, and called for his car and his retinue.

At Tenerife Sud Airport, a private jet owned by a Russian oligarch but permanently available for use by Russian military and Intelligence landed. Three very fit men, one with a military-style haircut, disembarked from the plane.

A driver was waiting in a black Mercedes 4x4. As soon as they completed formalities, they were in the car and it sped away to the south west.

***

I was on my way to the Finca. Natalia and Elvis were on their way to the airport.

I approached the turn-off that led to the farmhouse. It was at that distance above sea level where alpine-type trees proliferate and the house was obscured until you were up close.

Exiting the car, I walked the fifty or so yards towards the farmyard. A path skirted the property, and I left the main driveway and walked down narrow track to the rear. The trees created a dense border, and I was able to conceal myself and watch the property.

I had been there a few minutes when, despite my tinnitus-covering music, I heard talking: female, quiet, almost whispered. I couldn't work out where it was coming from at first. Then two men came around the back of the house, carrying bottles of water, a couple of loaves and packets of what I took to be cheese.

They opened a large door leading to a cellar. As the door opened, I realised where the whispering had been coming from. The girls were imprisoned in the cellar. It was feeding time.

The two men entered the cellar, down several steps, shouting in an Eastern European language. I saw the girls cowering, clearly terrified. I got out my phone. The signal was weak.

I tried to phone Uzcudzen and couldn't get through. I realised I would be pushing my luck if I thought I could get back to the car undetected. And I could hear them knocking the girls about.

I made my move. As fast as my dodgy legs would let me, I got to the side of the cellar door. One of the men started up the stairs to leave. As he reached the top of the stairs, I swung the hardwood stick with every bit of strength I could muster. It hit him across his forehead. He went down like a stone.

I felt the gun press into the back of my head.

'Who the fuck are you?' It was the third man. I was screwed, except that the sight of the first guy flat out inspired the females to riot. No matter how tough you are, being attacked by seven desperate women is a difficult situation to get out of.

They were all over gangster number two. My main preoccupation was staying alive.

The third guy was trying to see past me into the cellar, when his arm exploded. He had been hit by a bullet from a well-aimed standard issue Russian pistol. The man responsible for this excellent piece of marksmanship emerged from the woods alongside two companions. All three were masked, in black, all three of them pointing weapons and oozing competent menace.

I froze and raised my arms as the girls started to leave the cellar, gangster number two having been rendered unable to contribute further to the fight.

One of the men in black spoke. 'Irana!'

One of the girls, a beautiful if dishevelled blonde, reacted to his voice, and through the mask, recognized her brother.

'Leo!' She ran to him and he holstered the gun to embrace her. The other two men didn't move an inch, and I was still in their sights.

The loudspeaker broke through the chatter, in English.

'This is Colonel Paulino Uzcudzen of the Guardia Civil. You are surrounded. We are armed and about to enter the finca. Put down your weapons.'

One of the masked men spoke to me.

'Do you know him?'

'Yes, he is the head of the detectives.'

'Tell him to wait.'

Part of my disability is an inability to shout. I asked if I could go to the corner of the house so I could communicate better. The man pointed with his gun.

'If you run, you die.'

'Paulino, wait two minutes. It's me, Danny. It's under control – wait two minutes, please.'

'Is that you, Danny? What the hell are you doing here?'

'I can explain, Paulino. Just wait two minutes before you approach.'

I turned to face the gunman in time to see him disappear into the bushes heading downhill. So had his two companions and the two Russian girls, leaving five others and three gangsters, one badly wounded and two unconscious. The Russians had been courteous enough to line the girls up against the wall and had laid the injured gangsters, appropriately tie-wrapped, face down on the gravel.

'OK, Paulino. Everything's under control. Come in when you are ready.'

Just in case there were any trigger-happy cops accompanying Uzcudzen, I placed my hands on the wall and waited. The place filled with armed police, both Guardia Civil and local cops.

Uzcudzen walked up with his ever-present Praetorians. Looking down at the incapacitated thugs and the young women lined up, he laughed.

'Very neat, Danny.'

'Thanks, Colonel. When we have time, I would like to discuss the meaning of the English word surrounded.'

Further down the steep hill, along seldom used tracks, five Russian citizens drove towards the motorway, the airport and home.

***

I sat with Cabrera, Uzcudzen and Ronnie in the quiet lounge at the Duck. I had showered, topped up the painkillers and was cooling down with a couple of beers.

Uzcudzen told us that the gangsters were singing like birds. I suspected but never really knew that these were the three named by Natalia as being Elvis's "friends". They were low-level druggies recruited as gofers for Lawrie Binnet.

The three men were looking at long-term jail time and were doing all they could to mitigate their sentences. The girls were in the process of being repatriated and their Consuls had taken charge of them.

The murder of Binnet was still unresolved.

'I assume the Russians killed him,' I offered.

'They must have had a man in place before the extraction team arrived – we know that the jet they travelled in arrived after Binnet died.'

'I always thought Binnet was a ponce,' said Ronnie. 'I never realised he was into this stuff with the girls.'

Uzcudzen told me he would send someone down the next day to take my statement. I guess I must have looked a bit worn; my knees had taken a bit of a hammering. It didn't take much to rev them up. When Uzcudzen had left, Wendy joined us, and I was subjected to a lecture on how I really should avoid getting into these scrapes.

I confirmed that I would.

We ate, and I left them as the darkness dropped as it does so quickly in the Canaries. I wended my way back to the office, just to check the post and clear my desk.

Cabrera had installed a small CCTV camera near the door – the monitor was clearly visible from either of our desks. I saw a figure of a small man slowly approaching the door. I saw him knock, even as I heard him.

Even in the dark, the colour cameras seemed to pick out the varying hues of his face, accentuated by a different if equally garish tie to the one I had first seen him wearing. I opened the door, and he came in. I pointed to a chair, he sat down.

'I'm afraid my investigation into the whereabouts of the Russian Elvis impersonator went a little astray.'

'I know – please do not be concerned. All has worked out well.' He smiled. 'Mr Mclinden, I am authorized to pay you your fee and a substantial bonus.'

'Why? Elvis and Natalia are long gone.'

'I regret that you have been the victim of a hoax, perpetrated by me. I only arrived in Tenerife a few days ago, from Moscow.'

I was standing, looking down at this little man with the loud tie and colourful face. I thought I had better sit down to hear what was coming.

'My name is Artur Probka. I am Russian.'

Artur Probka or Arthur Corker had no discernible accent. I had thought him as British as me.

'I had been sent to look for a missing person – a Russian girl. She had been on a one-year break from her studies and had decided to join her friend, also a student, who was coming to work and have fun in Spain. They travelled together to Tenerife. I only found out two days ago that the second girl was the niece of a very prominent Russian politician.'

I stared at Probka, who sat down in the chair facing my desk.

'Initially I thought that someone based locally like you would speed up my enquiries. Actually, that was not necessary, as unknown to me, messages had been received in Moscow from the girls, from which their location was discovered.'

I nodded. That solved the mystery of where the black-clad Russians had come from. Probka continued.

'We knew of some Russians in Tenerife who could help us – we found one, the Russian Elvis, who had links to Binnet your countryman. Elvis knew something was going on with girls being kept in a farmhouse – he told me he had been asked to help secure them.'

'So he was never missing, then?'

'He also gave me Binnet's name and office address. I went to see Binnet – I got into his office through a fire escape. He was with a woman – they had photos of the girls on the desk, I threatened them with gun, and he told me where girls were.'

Probka's accent became more noticeable as his story became more dramatic.

'The woman was like wildcat, she attacked me, I slugged her and left her in passageway, taking the photos with me. I couldn't take the chance that Binnet might contact his jailors and tell them to dispose of the girls. So, I shot him in the head and left.'

'I was in the reception when all this happened,' I gasped.

'I realised this when I saw you come out of fire escape. You are very efficient, Danny Mclinden. I did not expect your investigation to move so quickly or to be so close behind me.'

I was looking into the eyes of a trained and capable assassin. He had already told me he had killed; he didn't seem in the least concerned at what I might do with this information.

I took a deep breath as he reached into his inside pocket. He pulled out an envelope and passed it to me. It contained a thousand Euros in fifties.

A car pulled up outside. It was a Mercedes, with blacked-out rear windows.

'My car is here to take me to the airport. Please come with me. There is someone who wants to speak to you. Don't worry – the driver will take you to wherever you need to be after he drops me off.'

I sat next to Probka in the luxurious 4x4 as we drove out of the Golf, heading towards the motorway that leads to the airport within a few minutes.

Leaning forward, he activated the tv screen in front of me. A face appeared which was familiar to all who follow Russian politics: Dmitry Medvedev, former President, now Prime Minister of Russia.

'Mr Mclinden, I understand you have been instrumental in the freeing of two female Russian citizens from the clutches of evil gangsters. I am informed you placed yourself in the danger to effect this rescue. Mr Probka, who sits alongside you, informs us that you are not in good health, which makes your efforts even more commendable. I realise that the temptation to tell others about this conversation may be overwhelming, but I would point out that it is barely believable and may undermine your credibility with whoever you recount it to.'

I nodded, swallowing, scarcely able to believe that this was happening, even after a chain of highly improbable events.

'Be aware that one of the young women you rescued is the daughter of a hero of Russia whose brother is a serving officer – the other is my niece, Lia. My country and my family are indebted to you, Mr Mclinden. A sum of money in excess of that given to you by Mr Probka will be paid into your bank account next week. If ever you are in difficulty, Danny, feel free to contact me or Mr Probka via our Consul. You are a friend of Russia. Thank you.'

The screen went dead. I was speechless. The car pulled up outside Departures. Probka shook my hand.

'Goodbye, Danny. It was a pleasure.'

I got dropped off at my villa. It was midnight. The Cessna that flew out over the Golf that I watched from my garden was undoubtedly the one carrying my new friend Artur Probka back to the snows of Moscow.

**

I slept well. A swim, followed by a full English at the Duck, set me up for one last duty regarding this case. I phoned Uzcudzen.

'Paulino, how many men have you got on the Binnet murder?'

'Quite a few, Danny. It's quite a puzzle.'

'Send them home, Paulino, then tell me where you want to take me for lunch. I've got a story for you.'

Part Three

Chapter Seventeen

The plume of dense black smoke carried out to sea by the wind appeared to come from Mount Teide, but it was actually one of the strange manifestations of the wind caused by the swirls of one of the many weather systems that operate over the island of Tenerife.

The fire had started in a large warehouse in the industrial sector of St Miguel de Abona, adjoining the motorway that bisects Golf del Sur and Amarilla from the commercial areas further up the foothills. The smoke was strong and acrid, and it took the resources of all the fire fighters in the south, with support coming from as far as Santa Cruz to put the blaze out.

I had seen the smoke and when I drove past the scene a few hours later, the firemen were still damping down. The warehouse was gutted – literally burnt to the ground. Arson was mentioned in social media, but without any factual support. The matter soon became filed away in the minds of the locals as well as the records of the emergency services.

Later that day, Cabrera and I were working in the office. It was a hot day, made tolerable by the seemingly ever-present breeze and helped by two glasses of iced tea Wendy had sent from over the road at the Tame Duck.

Cabrera was listening to the soccer commentary while working on his laptop, no doubt fiddling some figures. In my ears, from my opera collection, Pavarotti was singing a selection from *Martha*. What a voice.

I had a surprise visitor: Sergeant Primero Oliva, an experienced and competent member of the detective division of the Guardia. I had met him when I had first arrived in the Golf, when the money I had acquired was sitting in sports bags in my bedroom. My life had been very different. A few years had gone by since then.

Oliva sat in the visitor's chair between me and Cabrera. I got the impression that he wasn't a big fan of Cabrera, and Guillermo took the hint. He wandered off towards the Duck, taking the empty glasses with him.

Oliva produced a photograph: a man in his mid-thirties, thin, pinched cheeks. He looked rough, maybe a druggie.

'Do you know this guy, Danny?' The man in the photo looked familiar, but I couldn't place him at first.

'Maybe, let me think.'

'He is a very low-level drug dealer, a Brit – also illegal taxi driving, anything to scratch a living – frequents the Patch and Veronicas in Playa de Las Americas. We have him in custody – he assaulted a cop. When he was arrested, he had a large amount of Class A baggies on him.'

'How can I help?'

'He is asking to see you.'

I looked at the photo again. He looked familiar, but from another time, another place. I just couldn't figure out where.

'Why me?'

'He won't say. He refuses a lawyer, but has a right under Spanish law to consult with a third party – he wants you.'

Later, I drove to the police station in St Miguel de Abona, just a few miles from where I lived. Oliva was waiting for me and together, we went to a small cell in the basement of the building. It was situated at a lower level than the others – obviously high security. I entered and Oliva left me alone with the prisoner.

'Hello, Danny. Thanks for coming,' the prisoner said, in a London accent.

I looked at him hard, still not registering. He was thin, haggard, with stubble on his chin, wearing shabby, scruffy clothes.

'It's Don Brown, mate. You showed me round for a few weeks when I joined the job.'

Realization dawned. He had been a probationer Constable, just before I got promoted to CID. I hadn't seen him for years. I didn't know him well but before my accident, I'd understood that he was well thought of and doing a good job.

'Bloody hell, Don, what happened to you?'

'Joined the Drug squad, mate. I've been undercover for two and a half years. Been assigned to Interpol, Europol, DEA, you bloody name it. Currently I'm disowned by every fucker.'

'Why?'

'Admin,' he laughed. 'My handler changed recently. The new one is either useless or bent. All I know is that I was hung out to dry with a target on my back. The only way to get safe was to get locked up so I punched a copper after making sure I had five wraps of coke in my pocket.'

He leaned closer.

'Danny, I was working on a gang of importers using a warehouse in St Miguel de Abona to store product and money. They used to be tied up with the Venezuelans, but since they got taken down, the importers took over their operation and I suspect they're dealing directly with Columbia. So much coke's been getting into Spain through Algeciras and Valencia that the market's overloaded.'

My eyes widened. I thought the Venezuelans had been dangerous. They sounded like nothing compared with these guys.

'They've had to use the Canaries to store the stuff until demand picks up. Also, they were storing a mountain of cash. I passed the same info on three times. Someone was either incompetent or corrupt – in any case, nothing happened.'

'What did you do?'

'I burned the warehouse down.'

***

Spain is the main entrepot for Columbian-grown cocaine into Europe. The huge increase in availability came as a result of the Columbian government and the FARC guerrillas signing an armistice. Also, the collapse of neighbouring Venezuela's border controls has led to easy access to the coast for the numerous boats and ships that transport the product across the ocean to the waiting fast speedboats that make the run to shore.

Prices have crashed. Where a kilo would have cost £35,000 it is now down to about £25,000. All the Spanish ports are involved in this illegal trade, from Algeciras to Barcelona and along the coast of Galicia, the traditional gateway.

The United Kingdom is the third largest consumer of cocaine in the world, with 2.3% of the population being consumers, compared to Spain's 2%.

However, Great Britain is not on the main drugs highway: it is a terminus. Spain is a halfway house.

***

In Andalusia, the main gang was Moroccan and very dangerous. The Moroccans stepped into the breach left by the Venezuelans, and were linked with Kosovar and Albanian gangs based in Valencia, and Serbs based in Barcelona.

Together, these gangs directly controlled the eastern seaboard of the Atlantic, through the North Sea to Scandinavia.

The over supply problem was being tackled back in Columbia by restricting the harvest to two or three times a year, down from the previous five or six. In the meantime, the product was being stored and, as many of their usual facilities on the mainland were full, alternatives were found in the Canaries.

To compound the problem, there was a problem with laundering the cash. A huge effort by international law enforcement bodies had led to banks being closed, fined, and subject to intense scrutiny. As a result, cash had piled up and was being stored alongside the coke.

***

The guard brought in a couple of bottles of water, and a plastic chair for me. I sat down on it slowly – my knees were giving me trouble.

Don lit a cigarette and leaned back in his chair.

'How did you know I was on the island? I asked.

'After your accident, I kept in touch with a couple of the cops you worked with in the UK. The last I heard, you'd been dumped here by your lovely wife and had decided to settle.'

He was obviously relieved to have someone to talk to.

'Who were you reporting to?'

'There is a multi-agency task force with offices in Malmo, Sweden, and in Cadiz – trying to tackle the Moroccans. I was reporting to a woman called Olsen in Malmo. The Moroccans are based there, using Swedish passports. They travel in and out of Spain as they wish – they arrange transport for the coke all along the Atlantic seaboard. Antwerp mostly, before they move massive amounts to UK. They use some of the smaller French ports to get the coke to Paris – then all the way into Scandinavia and the Baltic. It was their stuff that was stored here. I kept hearing this name, Kadar. It seems he's the top man.'

What happened later was proof of the accuracy of Don Brown's work. There was indeed a man called Kadar.

'Why do you say there was a target on your back?'

'I was working for the Narcos. My job was to drive to a pickup point, collect baggies and then drive them to the street distributors in the holiday places. The pickup point changed daily. One day, I followed the guys who had delivered to me and they went to the warehouse. I sent the info to Malmo, got no response, tried again next day. That evening, I went to the pickup point I had been told to go to and no one showed. Then I got a message to report to the warehouse in St Miguel de Abona. There were no orders from Malmo. It was either a promotion or a problem, so I went.'

Don glanced at me nervously.

'I recognized some of the guys, as I was used to collecting from them,' he said. 'They were OK with me, so I thought it must be a promotion. We were wrapping money in clingfilm and storing it – there was millions. And pallets full of wrapped cocaine, dozens of them. Three Moroccans were overseers, tooled up with machine pistols and sidearms and supervising things from a raised walkway that went all the way around the place.'

Don leaned forwards on the bench in the cell to confide in me.

'Halfway through the shift, I asked if I could go for a piss and a smoke. They pointed me to a door. I walked through to the toilet and there was another Moroccan standing guard there. I went to the urinal and heard the swish of metal on leather as he pulled out the Glock from its holster. So it wasn't a promotion after all. I span around and pissed on the guy's feet. He was holding the gun to my head. His feet getting wet distracted him and I got him with a good left hook that floored him. I took the gun and used it to batter him unconscious, maybe worse.'

My eyes widened, but I didn't say anything to Don.

'I took his hat, put the holster and his shirt on and walked out of the room. The other Moroccans were all standing together on a raised walkway, facing the door I had gone through. They were obviously waiting for their pal to send me off the heavenly choir, from a place where they could keep a close eye on the other packers. Putting on the gunman's gear bought me ten seconds before they realised their man was down and I was escaping.'

'You made it, then?'

'I heard a shout and looking up, saw them starting to level their guns. I opened up with the Glock and broke into a run towards the exit door. They responded in panic, spraying bullets all over the place, All the packers hit the deck as I hit the outer door with my shoulder. It was steel with a Remington lock – I had to shoot the lock out before I could kick it open.'

'They must have suspected something?' I asked.

'The only way thing that could have caused their reaction was if someone had told them I was an undercover cop. My cover was blown. I got to my car as the packers in the warehouse hit the pavements. They were panicking. In the back of my car was a can of petrol. I always carry a few extra litres, just in case. I tore the cap I had taken from my would-be assassin and stuffed it into the opening. I set it on fire with my lighter, ran back towards the open door and threw the improvised Molotov cocktail onto the pile of cash that was stored in the centre of the warehouse floor. The Moroccans were shooting in panic – they'd shot holes in some of the drums that contained ether. The fire caught immediately. The gunmen were now in the car park, looking for me – and the packers had legged it.'

'So what did you do?'

'Once they saw the flames through the open doors, they tried to go back in. I shot one dead centre – the other two backed off as the warehouse exploded and following another shot that emptied the magazine, they ran off.'

'You've had quite a day,' I said.

'I drove to Playa, got some baggies from a street dealer, hailed down a patrolling Guardia Civil car and punched the smaller guy of the two-man crew. I got a good hiding, a comfy cell and a half-decent cheese and ham baguette. Now I'm either safe, or I'm waiting for some paid-off member of the Guardia to walk in and blow my head off.'

I checked my phone. We were underground and the reception was poor. I told Don that I would go and make a phone call to Uzcudzen. I called the guard and was allowed out, the cell door clanging behind me. I heard the lock turn.

At the top of the stairs, Sergeant Oliva sat waiting for me. He was about fifty, that age when many cops are either thinking impatiently of retirement and a quiet life, or were terrified of leaving a profession and a way of life that was in imbued in them.

The excitement, occasional danger, extremes of elation or disappointment was addictive to some, but was exhausting to others.

I decided to gamble on Oliva being an adrenaline addict,

'The guy is an undercover British cop attached to Europol. His cover has been blown and he fears assassination, possibly from bent cops.'

Oliva stood and looked at me incredulously. He walked me into a side room, my stick tapping on the marble floor. The station was in the middle of a shift change, the off-duty guys laughing and joking with those coming on duty. I saw the cell-guard going off duty. He handed keys to a younger man.

'This cannot be true, Danny.'

'If you'd heard what I've just heard, I think you would believe it, Sergeant.'

The new cell guard and one other cop hurriedly started down the stairs towards the cells. In the very bottom cell, awaiting his fate, sat Don Brown.

'Who's the relief jailer?'

'There are a couple of new guys from La Laguna here today, why?'

'He seems in an awful hurry, and why are two men needed down there?'

Oliva got to his feet and started down the stairs. I followed him. There were handrails on both sides, and I placed my stick under my arm and swung down behind him, enabling me to keep up. Don's cell door was open. I could hear men struggling.

'Dejalo solo détente o disparo!' shouted Oliva, unholstering his Beretta.

As he turned right to enter the cell, there was a gunshot and Oliva went down in the corridor. My momentum carried me over his body and I turned to face the shooter. As I did, Don, who was being held in a stranglehold, managed to kick out and unbalance the man with the gun.

I spun my stick and with both hands, brought it down on the back of the gunman's head. Don managed to throw his head back and catch the strangler full on his nose. As he fell back, releasing Don, the corrupted cop went for his pistol. It had just left the holster when Oliva, blood pumping from his shoulder, shot him dead.

Oliva slumped in the corner, badly hurt. I went over to him.

'Get the other gun, Danny, and take mine. Trust no one here. Get out quick, go to Uzcudzen.'

Don took the gun from the hand of the dead man. I took the one from the man I had clubbed and Oliva's. We started upstairs. It couldn't have been worse timing – it was still the shift change, so two full contingents of cops were in or near the station. We could hear them reacting to the gunshot and footsteps approaching the door at top of the stairs. I put my two Berettas in my pockets.

'Take me prisoner.'

'What?'

'Get the gun, hold it to my head and walk me out. My car is straight outside.'

Don got behind me and held the beretta to my forehead. 'Keep back or I'll shoot him.' The cops stepped back.

We reached the main door to the police station and pushed our way through.

'Close the door,' Don shouted. Someone did so, leaving most of the cops inside. There were a few cops outside, their guns trained on us. I opened the door of the car with the remote. I got into the driving seat, Don sat behind me, with the gun still at my head.

I hit the accelerator and we sped away. Thank god for the self-discipline of the well-trained Guardia Civil.

The blue lights were visible behind us as we sped down the mountain towards the motorway. I phoned Uzcudzen, I asked him to call off the posse and I would come to wherever he wanted me, as long as I was meeting him.

Paulino is a tough, decisive hombre, and he didn't disappoint. Within a few minutes, I could see the police cars slowing and parking as he barked his instructions over the police radio, allowing me to slow down.

I found out later that Oliva, despite his wound, had managed to get to a radio and was also issuing the 'back off' instruction to his colleagues.

I drove inland, to the observation point. Uzcudzen was standing by his car. His retinue behind him, they were all carrying serious artillery, armoured vests and Kevlar helmets, even the Chief of Detectives himself.

I told Don to pass me the two Berrettas we had taken from the assassins and Oliva. I placed them, along with mine, in full view on the shelf behind the windscreen. Then, with hands showing, I got out of the car.

My legs were useless. Two trips up and down the cell steps had sent them into spasm. Without my stick, I struggled to walk. The cops had their guns levelled at us.

'Do you vouch for your companion, Danny?'

'I do vouch for him, Paulino.'

'Then put down your hands.'

He nodded and one of his men went to their car and brought out the African hardwood cane that had dealt with

Don's would-be killer. I had dropped it as Don and I left the Police station. It was becoming known by the Detective division of the Guardia Civil in as the weapon of choice for crippled Private Detectives. He gently passed it to me and I thanked him.

'How is Sergeant Oliva?' I asked.

'In surgery as we speak. Prognosis is good.'

'He saved our lives, Paulino.'

'He says you saved his.'

'Well, let's call it a team effort.'

Paulino laughed. So did his retinue. If he hadn't, they wouldn't have.

We sat in Uzcudzen's car and Don recounted the story he had told me.

'Who were the assassins?'

'Two serving Guardia Civil officers. How they managed to be scheduled to work at that particular station together is being looked into – it looks as though we have a number of rotten apples. We will find them – the one you disabled is a little concussed. When he recovers, he will talk to me.'

From the look in the Chief of Detective's eye, I knew this to be true.

We talked for a while. Uzcudzen explained to me that he feared the situation Don Brown was involved in indicated there was a serious problem and that the Moroccan drug cartel had infiltrated the Europol intelligence system.

He was worried that as I had helped Don, I had made myself into a target for the Moroccans. He had already arranged a permit for me, legalizing the guns I had stored following the kidnap of Mrs Cabrera. I could now carry them concealed. Regarding Don, Uzcudzen was in a quandary.

'I'm going to make a show of taking Don to the internment facility at Reina Sofia airport. In a few minutes, two black 4x4s will arrive. They will go front and back around me and off we will go. Ask Don to get into the back of your car, cover him, and get him to the Marina. Wait for us to leave. Can you get Ronnie to take you to La Gomera on his boat? Whoever is working for the Moroccans will think we have Don in protective custody. You two can sit it out on Gomera until things settle down.'

He passed us each one of the Berettas and six clips of ammunition. 'I hope you don't need them.'

***

Ronnie rang me to tell me he was ready. His small yacht was similar to dozens of pleasure boats that enter and leave the harbour each day.

I drove to the parking area near the shops and cafés and saw Ronnie waiting. I told Don to follow me and we walked towards the craft, hoping no one would notice us. Ronnie started to cast off and within seconds of our feet hitting the deck, the boat was progressing towards the harbour mouth, with Don stashed safely below.

We cruised steadily through that nameless strait that separates La Gomera from Tenerife. First, we sailed down to Los Christianos and turned west, off Playa. We passed the tourist hotspots without incident. No one was following us at sea, so we quickly turned and headed directly to the island.

There are numerous small beaches and bays to anchor off. La Gomera. The one Ronnie chose must be the smallest. My legs hurt. Rather than chance being lowered into the small skiff, I preferred to lower myself into the sea and swim in, the water easing my weight and taking the pressure from the knees. Don followed in the skiff containing the guns and ammo.

Typically of Ronnie, he had asked Wendy to prepare a packed lunch and a flask of hot coffee each. It was as though we were going on a day trip to the seaside, not trying to escape a team of ruthlessly efficient killers. He did, however, have the foresight to include the machine pistol I had stored in the Tame Duck's safe.

When Ellen Perez had 'borrowed' this deadly bit of kit from the police property store, I had jokingly said she also took enough ammo for a small war. A small war was exactly what we were eventually heading for.

From the beach, there was a narrow path leading to a promontory and a dirt road. On that road sat a man in a Land Rover, arranged by Wendy. This was our transport to what would turn out to be temporary safety. My tinnitus started up, so I put my ear pods in. Paul Mcartney was singing 'I Don't Know'. *Neither do I*, Sir Paul, *neither do I.*

Chapter Eighteen

Abdel Kadar was a handsome man. Born in Marrakesh, his grandfather had been a prominent politician, benefactor to the poor and an international hashish smuggler.

His father had died while he was a baby, so Abdel was brought up by his loving but strict grandfather, his mother becoming a servile and increasingly peripheral figure in his young life.

The old man insisted on the boy getting the best education. Private tutors nurtured an inherent talent for languages and by the time he was ten, Abdel was as comfortable speaking English, French, and Spanish as he was his native tongue. He was able to get by conversationally in Russian and even had a smattering of Mandarin.

Abdel had other skills: he was a visionary, vigorous, criminal entrepreneur. By the time he was in his twenties, he was already taking over his grandfather's supply routes and moving from the hashish business into the acquisition, storage, and distribution of cocaine, which was vastly more profitable.

He built on his grandfather's contacts to expand the part of the supply route that started in North Africa and ended up in every city, town, and village in western Europe, where the cool and trendy middle classes supplemented their ever-growing desire to blot out the reality of their existence by snorting a powerful stimulant that those same idiots sought to normalise by calling it acceptable names.

Blow, Coke, Charlie, Wash, Toot. It made them feel confident, staved off sleep, made them excited and happy. It also made them sweat, made their hearts beat faster, made them shit more and become paranoid.

Abdel also set about extending his supply chain back to Columbia and Venezuela. Initially, he had relied on Venezuelan middlemen. From bases on the Venezuelan Atlantic coast, they had established routes and coordinated the deliveries of product across the Atlantic to several destinations under Abdel's control in southern Europe, but with a number of fall-back, alternative storage facilities in the Canaries, West Africa, and the Azores.

His relationship with the Venezuelans had been deteriorating for a while. They had not been good partners. They had become greedy. Abdel decided to seek alternative partners and made contact directly with the Columbians.

As these negotiations were going on, something happened in Tenerife. The Venezuelans sought to recover a paltry sum of money, but their efforts ended in chaos, with their whole Canary Islands operation shut down and about twenty of the Venezuelans in a Spanish jail. There was some story about an English cripple setting them all up, but he wasn't interested. It suited him that the Venezuelans had been mopped up.

The Venezuelans' greed had resulted in them driving the Columbians to overproduce. Harvests had gone from three per year to six. As a result, supply exceeded demand and prices had dropped. Now he had been divested of the Venezuelans, Abdel was able to convince the Columbians to hold back on production whilst he ran down stock stored in warehouses situated in Tenerife, near the access points to mainland Spain.

Tenerife. The place kept coming up. The fire that had destroyed his warehouse, one of his best overseers shot dead, and that problem when the Venezuelans had been mopped up. The warehouse had originally been theirs. He looked at the island on a map. Tenerife was small place, well positioned for holding product. He decided to pay a visit, but first, he had business in Sweden.

***

The Land Rover moved slowly along the track. There aren't many roads on La Gomera and speeding along them is not a good idea: it upsets the locals, draws attention, and may end up with you dangling over some cliff edge that, had you been driving carefully, you may have anticipated earlier.

Juan, our driver, was ex-military, getting on, bit of a belly, and with a skin like mahogany tanned in the tortured ravines and defiles of this ancient volcanic landscape.

Where he was driving us wasn't at first clear, only that it was high, tortuous to get to, and remote. Eventually, we emerged from the dense surroundings of trees and bushes into a clearing within which was a building, an old farm or manor house.

He parked some yards from the door and got out. Juan placed his fingers in his mouth and let out a low whistle. He waited, and soon, another whistle signalled a response, from inside the house. A door opened and out stepped a younger man, who beckoned us forward.

'Is OK - he is my son.'

We entered the house, which was dark and cool. Small, shuttered windows kept out the light and more importantly, the heat. The walls were local stone, thick and strong enough to stop a tank. Juan nodded to the younger man who left the building. I heard a motorbike start up and drive off.

Juan settled us in. We ignored the upstairs rooms. Two single beds had been set up in a small room. There was a kitchen, stocked with bread, cereal, milk, and other basics. A couple of large batteries provided any electric power we may need. There was bottled gas, for light, and to fuel the cooker.

'I come back every two days, bring food. New battery, maybe gas.'

Juan passed me a two-way radio with a charger. He kept the other handset.

'I will call when I'm a few minutes away. Phone works, but not reliable.'

He shook our hands and walked to the Land Rover. As he did, he placed his hand to his mouth and let out a whistle. He waited and from some distance away, the whistle was returned.

Sibo Gomero, also known as El Sibo, is whistled Spanish, used by native La Gomerans to communicate across the narrow valleys and deep ravines that radiate through the island. It can be used over a range of up to about three and a half miles. This was the method Juan used to tell his son that he was leaving, maybe telling to open the beer, maybe a warning not to shoot him as he drove down the track towards the sea.

Don and I set about making the place secure. The stairs leading from the first floor, we filled with furniture: heavy Spanish-made chairs and tables. They wouldn't stop anyone coming down them if attackers managed to get in from the first floor, but they would certainly slow them down. We boarded the rear door and windows. If they wanted us, they would have to come through the front where we had a direct line of fire.

***

Uzcudzen's convoy drove to the detention area within the Reina Sophia airport. One of his men had a blanket over his head and, held by two colleagues, was ushered into the reception area and from there, direct to a secure cell.

To all intents and purposes, the undercover English cop who had destroyed millions in cash and stored cocaine, was now safely interred in protective custody. For the next few hours, Uzcudzen's men, including the Don Brown impersonator, slipped out of the complex one by one. Until, by late evening, the facility was down to the usual minimal security staffing levels the facility had when it wasn't in active use.

***

In Malmo, Sweden, Abdel Kadir sat in his penthouse overlooking the city centre. He owned the block, which was rented to high-end Swedish and international professionals. He retained the penthouse for his exclusive use.

Tonight, he had invited a particularly important female guest. His tastes in women were not what you would expect from a man brought up in a culture where women were second-class citizens, where his own mother had been marginalized, and he had no sisters.

He was a ruthless and merciless killer, or rather ordered others to be on his behalf. He had never been in any form of serious relationship, refusing to get into any arranged marriage as was the norm, and avoiding even the thought of starting a family. Instead, he hired exclusive escorts whom he would wine and dine and talk to. Usually, the evening would end in bed, but not always. He was a careful and considerate lover, a respectful and attentive host. It was as though this civilized behaviour was an antidote to the mayhem, cruelty and blood that permeated every day of his life. However, on this night, although the reason for the date was romantic for his guest, for him, it was strictly business.

The lady visiting his apartment tonight was a blonde, fit but not beautiful; about five feet eight in height. She was wearing an Oscar de la Renta dress he'd given to her as a gift on their previous date. The chef who had been hired exclusively for them that evening had two Michelin stars, and the waiter was highly experienced and very discreet.

A bottle of Krug Clos d'Ambonnay champagne was chilled to perfection in the ice bucket as Abdel Kadir took his visitor's hand and led her to the table.

On her table mat sat a small, exquisitely wrapped package. He invited her to open it. Inside the jewellery box was a pair of Angara ruby tear drop earrings. Her intake of breath at their beauty belied her naivety. She could see they were expensive, but not the 600,000 Krona they actually cost. He asked her to put them on. She sat, clearly impressed. She obviously wasn't used to these opulent surroundings, or this amount of attention.

In fact, she was more used to the far more modest surroundings commensurate with an employee of the Malmo Police, even one on special assignment to Europol with duties that included monitoring and supporting undercover Police investigating drug smuggling throughout western Europe.

Kadar's phone rang. Despite the pretentiousness of his world, Kadar had a basic phone, one that could be disposed of quickly and easily on a weekly, sometimes daily basis.

He made his excuses and slipped into the marble-tiled bathroom.

It was his man in Tenerife. The undercover cop, exposed by a process of trial and error, had escaped. He had been picked up by Guardia Civil and taken straight to the airport. At first, they thought he had been flown straight back to UK but their informer within the Guardia now told them he was being held in the detention block at Reina Sofia.

Kadar was annoyed. He had flown to the northern limit of his empire to relax, recuperate, and continue to build his relationship with this woman who was about to supply him with the names, locations and details of every undercover cop working against him, and have a little fun. Still, this Tenerife bullshit still followed him. It was minor but irritating.

'How many men have you?'

'About twenty.'

'Arms?'

'Plenty.'

'Then attack the place, find this English bastard and kill him.'

'What about the local cops?'

'Kill them too – it's time they learned who is in charge. Don't phone me till it's done and not before morning.'

***

Uzcudzen returned to his office in Santa Cruz and after clearing his desk, went home. His wife met him with a couple of iced glasses of Tinto de Verano and they sat in the shade of the almond grove together. As usual, she told him about her day, and as usual, he studiously avoided doing the same.

As Mrs Uzcudzen went back inside to refill their glasses, he looked out over his olive trees and pondered the situation at work. He knew that the Europol Task Force had managed to place several undercover officers into the drug importing operations throughout Europe. The name Kadar had surfaced, the same name as the old Hashish dealer who had avoided the authorities for years. Could it be the same guy? Probably not, he would be far too old.

Clearly Don Brown was one of the undercover officers, and Don's cover was blown. Was this due to informers within the law enforcement community? Or had the dealers just worked out that there was someone working undercover on the island and that it was this particular Englishman?

One way or the other, Uzcudzen knew these Moroccans were violent, ruthless and unpredictable. He was worried. Events proved he was right to be.

***

Two minibuses pulled up at the gates of the freight entrance into the airport. The security guard came out and approached the driver. The silenced automatic pistol cracked and the guard fell, dead before he hit the floor.

A pair of men entered the gatehouse and after ensuring there were no more security staff in there, they opened the automatic gate and the barrier, allowing the minibuses access.

They sped directly to the detention facility, clearly with advanced knowledge of exactly where it was. They screeched to a halt and both buses emptied as armed men swarmed towards the entrance. An explosive device blew off the front door and the two Guardia Civil officers securing the premises were gunned down.

Ten men secured the perimeter of the building, ten others entered and started to search.

Vehicles sped towards the facility: the airport police and security, alarmed by the CCTV footage of the unknown minibuses heading across the airport tarmac, sounds of an explosion and a report of a security guard being shot down.

As the first security patrol vehicle approached the facility, one of the attackers opened fire with a machine gun. The van was riddled with bullets and the passenger was wounded, but the driver managed to spin the vehicle around and escape.

The other vehicles recognized the seriousness of the situation and the fact they were outgunned and backed off.

Soon, the attackers who had entered the building realised it was empty. Stepping over the corpses of the two dead cops, they re-boarded the minibuses and were soon joined by those who had been protecting the perimeter.

The buses sped out of the airport, pursued at a distance, by the security and police vehicles. As they drove up the hill leading to the motorway, the minibuses drew alongside each other, blocking each lane of the dual carriageway. The back doors flew open and machine guns opened fire on the pursuing vehicles.

With no firepower capable of responding, the uniforms stopped, and the minibuses drove off, unimpeded.

Chapter Nineteen

The next morning in Malmo, Brigit Olsen awoke to find her new lover preparing breakfast. All the staff had left the previous night. She had heard that Moroccan men were great lovers and she had not been disappointed. After her divorce, she had started to believe that she was unlikely to find love again. She had dated, usually through the internet, but had met no one that she could envisage having a long-term relationship with.

Then one afternoon, she had got into a conversation with a man in a supermarket. He was very well-dressed, obviously not used to doing his own shopping. He had asked her for help, and she had smilingly agreed to help him fill his basket.

By way of thanks, he invited her to join him in the store's coffee shop. In there, he admitted, laughing, that his shopping was normally done by one of his staff, but she was on holiday and for the first time in years, he was forced to fend for himself. He told her his name was Saad Othmani.

He asked to see her again. They had gone out twice. He told her he was involved in the oil business. Saad appeared fascinated by her work in the Police. She never really realised how much information she had divulged to him. Their primary target was a countryman of his. They knew his name, Kadar, but they had no photographs. He was a will o' the wisp, an enigma.

Saad told her he knew people in Morocco who might help – they would be very wary of engaging directly with law enforcement, but they would talk to him.

Brigit Olsen believed she was establishing an extremely worthwhile contact and a possible informant. To encourage him, she imparted even more information. She was being played.

Last night, he invited her into his world. She was blinded by the opulence, seduced by the luxury, corrupted by the con. He told her he was concerned not to involve people he might know in Morocco. She insisted that the authorities were only interested in this man Kadar. She explained the operation in detail. He took in every word: the infiltrations that had been made, where, when and how. Whilst she didn't name the undercover cops, she named some of Kadar's own employees.

Abdel was alarmed at how deep some of the undercovers had got, and relieved that some others had not got very far. She didn't really need to name names; it would be easy enough to work out who they were. His brain was quite capable of retaining virtually all the information. But just in case, every word was recorded on video.

***

Uzcudzen was watching a movie with his wife when his phone rang. There was a major incident at the airport: three dead. He was on his feet and heading for the door with the phone at his ear, his wife fastening on his ID badge and his holster. Before she inserted the gun, she checked the magazine was full and the safety was on. She had been a cop's wife for many years. She knew all about interrupted films and TV programmes, cancelled holidays, and disrupted family celebrations.

Paulino was a good husband and father. They had built a comfortable home together and family together. She loved and appreciated him and was prepared to make the sacrifices necessary for him to build a career. He could not have done it without her.

Uzcudzen slipped on his hi viz uniform jacket, kissed her cheek and jumped into his car. He affixed the blue light to the top of his BMW 7 series and sped along the motorway to Reina Sofia. He found chaos – ambulances and police cars creating a sea of blue lights. He soon established that the wounded had been or were being transported to hospital. The dead remained in situ, awaiting CSI and ultimately, the body carriers, to transport them to the morgue.

Paulino continued to the detention facility. Members of his personal staff were liaising with security staff and onsite Police. The consensus at first was that this was a terrorist attack. As the night wore on and the information clarified, Uzcudzen began to have doubts.

The attack had a very narrow focus. There were no suicide bombers, there was no focus on the terminal itself. The attackers had a target. That target was in the detention facility: that target was Don Brown.

Paulino had underestimated the ruthlessness and arrogant confidence of Kadar; also his capability to put a heavily-armed team into the field so quickly. By the sound of it, the Tenerife police could easily be outgunned and outmatched by the gunmen. He called the commander of the Grupo Especial de Operaciones on the mainland, heavily armed, highly trained Police specialists. They mobilized.

***

In Gomera, Don and I established a one-man-in-one-man-out system whereby we patrolled the grounds all the time. We found a roll of wire and established some trip traps in the undergrowth. We also found green string, specifically for garden use. Using old tins and bottles, we created an alarm system where if anyone touched the string, the bottles and cans would let us know someone was approaching.

***

Brigit Olsen felt as though she was floating as she drove towards her office. She had returned home after breakfast, packed away her expensive dress and put the earrings into her jewellery box. She had never been happier. She listened to the news on her car radio as she drove: a terrorist attack on an airport in Tenerife. Drugs and terrorism – she would never be short of work.

On her arrival, she greeted her co-workers in the high security wing of the Malmo Police office. Several noted the spring in her step, high colour, and good humour. The attack was mentioned. Several of her co-workers had spent holidays in the Canaries – what a world.

Brigit started catching up on her coded messages. She was running five undercovers directly and realised that in a job that required constant attention, she had been lax lately, due to her recent romantic entanglement. As she worked her way through the encryptions, she received a call from a colleague based in the southern European equivalent of her office.

'Hi Brigit, it's Ellen Perez.'

They had met a couple of times at a training course in Madrid and when Ellen had visited Malmo. They made small talk for a few minutes before Ellen got down to business.

'Brigit – we've had a serious incident in Tenerife. Three killed – two cops and a security guard. I've just had the local

Chief of Detectives on the phone asking if we've had any contact from the Tenerife undercover. I know you've registered his check calls, are you sure there were no messages?'

Brigit could feel her colour rising. There had been at least one encrypted message. She had assumed it was just the regular check call all undercovers were required to do at prescribed intervals. The check call was recorded on the main computer. It contained no detail, only the fact that the operative had checked in. It was Brigit's job to decode it and ensure no information was contained that needed further action.

'No, Ellen, nothing new or unusual – just the usual check-in, but I will check again.'

Ellen said her goodbyes. Brigit started to panic and immediately went to the messages. She de-encrypted and her panic increased. There were three messages, all of them from Don Brown, an English undercover placed in the Canary Islands, initially to infiltrate the British dealers but who had, according to these messages, managed to get to the Canarian root of the Kadir operation. They were calls for help, of increasing desperation. She had failed him.

If she admitted her laxity, she would certainly be removed from this department; she may be dismissed from the police. She didn't admit her mistake. She covered her arse – she deleted the messages and called Ellen back.

'Hi Ellen, I've checked – no content other than to check in – all seems fine.'

***

Ellen Perez was, of course, the policewoman whose sister was married to my erstwhile partner Cabrera. She had broken rules and laws in helping me to set her sister free from kidnappers some two years earlier.

I had become close to Ellen, but she regarded me rightly as a mess, damaged beyond repair. She was affectionate towards me in the way you would be with a three-legged dog. I had hoped for more, but it wasn't to be.

She had been promoted after the incident involving me and moved initially to Madrid, and soon afterwards to Cadiz, where she now headed the communications and administration unit in the Southern Europe branch of a multi-agency task force involved with the ever-ongoing fight against illegal drug trafficking.

Ellen often visited Tenerife to spend time with her family. She made time for me too. I looked forward to sipping a leche monchada or, at the right time of the day, a carajillo, in her company. Looking at those black eyes, and oh, that hair and thinking of another time, another place where she might have seen beyond the damage.

When Ellen finished her conversation with Brigit Olsen, she phoned Uzcudzen.

'I've spoken to the Swedish cop that was handling Don Brown. She says other than his check calls, he hasn't contacted her – his checks are all as expected.'

'How often does he check in?'

'Daily, between 0900 and 1300, as do the others.'

'And your contact says Brown is up to date.'

'Yes, all in order.'

'She is lying, Ellen. He has not contacted her for at least two days.'

***

Brigit Olsen finished her shift a worried woman. From the elation of the previous night, her mood had slumped. She had let down a colleague in the field.

She had always been a conscientious worker. Her recent romance had distracted her – for the first time since her divorce, there was something in her life more important than her career: she had a man in her life. She smiled as she remembered the ecstasy of the previous night, before her mind clouded again with thoughts of the undercover officer who relied on her and may now be in serious trouble.

She hadn't heard from her lover all day. Shortly after arriving home, he came to call, but he wasn't alone. The man she knew as Saad Othmaani smiled as she opened the door. She was a little unkempt, not yet changed from her working clothes.

'...I wasn't expecting to see you tonight.'

'You never know when I may appear.' There was a coldness about him.

His companion was, like him, of North African appearance. Kadar spoke to him abruptly. 'Show her.'

The companion took out an iPhone. He pressed play on a video. Brigit was in it, as was Kadar.

The video played a recording of Brigit imparting confidential information to Kadar, as she sat there in the dress he'd bought her.

'What is this, Saad?'

'Sit down, Brigit, you need to see it all.'

A time-lapse showed her entering the apartment, being given the earrings, wined, dined, seduced, and making love, as well as imparting confidential information. It was all there.

She watched herself wearing the precious earrings and drinking the world's most expensive champagne, before being led to the bed they'd shared and the gymnastics that followed. Brigit realised that she had, in every sense of the expression, been had.

'Watch it all, Brigit. This is to inform you that you now work for me. The dress I bought you cost $7,000; the earrings $50,000. The information you gave me is enough to send you to jail for at least ten years. A payment of another £50,000 was paid into your bank account an hour ago.'

Bridget was speechless. Her mouth opened in shock, but no words came out.

'You have been bribed, and imparted information that has led to the death of at least one undercover cop. You are going to tell me who the others are, or this will be sent to your bosses and the press all over Europe.'

She felt dizzy and weak, gripping the arms of her chair.

'Who are you?' she managed to ask.

'I am your nightmare. You will never see me again unless I decide to kill you, which will be a mercy if you fail to deliver whatever I ask you now or in the future. You may keep the dress, the money, and the jewellery. My name is Abdel Kadar. Congratulations, you are the only cop that knows who I am.'

***

The night dropped like a curtain. No moon, the only illumination coming from the myriad stars that glowed in the cloudless sky. Don had come in from a walk around the perimeter. I made tea and a couple of sandwiches. We took a couple of chairs outside and sat on the veranda as the daytime heat dissipated from the masonry and the ground.

We heard the motorbike, distant, climbing, on its way to us, then the two-way radio activated. It was Juan.

'My son is coming to you – he has a message.'

The young man chugged the bike up to the door. He passed me a phone. The text message came from Uzcudzen. It contained details of the attack on the airport, about the three dead, the fact that the whole undercover operation may be compromised and most worryingly for Don and me, the fact that about twenty heavily armed men were looking for us. He told us to stay put.

I passed the phone to Don. He read it, looking alarmed.

'Jesus Christ, this is getting hot, Danny.'

My thoughts went straight to the Golf. It wouldn't take a genius to work out that was the place to start looking for me. It was also logical to assume Kadar's men would think Don was with me. Only Uzcudzen, Ronnie and probably Wendy knew where we were. We were even staying off our phones. Unless someone told them, we were safe.

But we were dealing with people who needed to act fast. They must have known that despite their firepower, they would soon be faced with Spanish Special Forces. Their next step would be to go to the Golf, then they would head to the Duck.

***

Brigit Olsen put on the dress and the earrings she had been gifted. She transferred the contents of her bank account, including her savings and the $50,000 to an animal charity. She wrote several notes: one to her father, her sister, and an aunt she had been close to. The last letter she wrote was to her senior officer at Malmo Police HQ.

Tears ran down her face. She had been a failure as a wife and a daughter; her idiocy may have led to the deaths of brave undercover officers.

She walked out of the door of her apartment onto the balcony. She mounted a chair and looked over the wall to the ground below.

***

Don and I discussed the situation. We were in the wrong place, sitting on top of a mountain while people trying to protect us put themselves in the firing line. If these bastards were coming for us, so be it, no more hiding.

I radioed Juan and asked him to bring the Land Rover. I phoned Ronnie and told him what we feared. The cops would be running around all over the island. No one was protecting the Duck; we were coming back. Ronnie protested but he saw the truth of the danger. We would get a boat back into the Marina then get to the Duck as quickly as possible; he should lock up and wait for us.

Juan arrived and we got into the Rover. There were plenty of boats in the harbour that would sail us back to the marina. He contacted his son, by whistling, to arrange one.

***

In the Duck, as Ronnie was talking to me, business went on as normal. It was early evening, before the entertainment started. On the big screen TV, Watford were playing West Ham.

Sitting watching the game were about thirty men, including two former members of the Manchester City Guvnors and a huge man, a former member of the Leeds United Service crew. There was also Bunny, a former accountant, now the friend and business partner of the hooligans.

Elsewhere, in the quieter part of the bar, Mr and Mrs Cabrera were sharing an early dinner.

Two men entered. North African, unsmiling, they sat at the bar and ordered soft drinks. Wendy served them. With Ronnie watching, they asked Wendy a couple of questions. Leaving them, she walked down the bar to Ronnie.

'What did they want?' he whispered.

'Asking about Danny.'

'What did you say?'

'As we agreed, I told them he hasn't been in for a few days.'

Ronnie went outside. In the car park were two cars: four North Africans in one car, two in another. He lit a cigarette, just a bar manager having a quick break and a smoke. He took out his phone, ostensibly looking at his messages. Actually, he was messaging the hooligans.

Inside, the big Yorkshireman looked at his phone. He downed his pint and went to the bar for replenishment. Standing alongside the North Africans, he passed the pint glass to Wendy.

As he brought his elbow back, he hit the first man flush in the mouth, teeth blood and spittle emitting from his damaged mouth as he fell backwards from the bar stool. Without interrupting his movement, Yorkie continued to spin. Bringing his right hand in a half circle, he hit the second man full on the temple. He was unconscious before he hit the bar floor.

***

Don and I boarded the motor yacht and the steersman hit the accelerator. He had been told this was urgent and we shot across the channel at high speed.

I phoned Uzcudzen. He answered immediately. I told him what we were doing. He was dealing with a sighting of the terrorist group north of Santa Cruz.

'I'll bet you its false, Paulino. They are after Don and me and looking for an opportunity to cause chaos. Why would they go to the north? I think they're causing a diversion.'

'We have to check, Danny. I thought you were safely tucked away.'

Another call came in. It was Ronnie.

'Six in the car park. Yorkie's whacked two and they're stashed in the stock room. The others are bound to make a move soon.'

'We're twenty minutes away – try to stay safe.'

I phoned Uzcudzen again.

'It's the Duck – eight of them – six sat in the car park, two detained in the storeroom.'

I heard him shout down the Police radio to abandon the search – everyone to head to Golf del Sur.

'Danny, we will be thirty minutes.'

***

In Malmo, Brigit Olsen teetered on the chair. Her depression and self-loathing had totally taken over, for a moment then.

She thought about the earrings. It would be a shame to see them packed away in the mortuary. She should sell them and raise even more money for the animal charity.

Brigit got down from the chair, then she reflected on her career. She had done good things. Her husband was an arsehole; she had been conned by this Moroccan slimeball. Why should she die? So what if she got fired and went to prison? She could bring Kadar down first.

She put on her coat, walked into Malmo Police HQ and into her supervisor's office. She closed the door behind her and sat down.

***

The Duck started to empty. Ronnie controlled the flow, two at a time. Wendy let a few out of the back.

In the storeroom, two bloodied North Africans sat in the corner, tie-wrapped and gagged. My partner Guillermo Cabrera stood guard with a hammer in his hand. Next to him stood the fearsome Mrs Cabrera, no hammer necessary. A nervous but determined Bunny made up a trio of jailers.

The two Mancs had taken the men's pistols and took positions at the entrances, one behind Ronnie, one behind Wendy, awaiting the inevitable attack.

Ronnie had taken the Glock I had stored in the safe and stuck it into his belt.

***

The speedboat entered the harbour at twice the permitted speed, causing the harbour master's entire workforce to run down the jetty to remonstrate with us. The sight of the machine pistol in my hand and the two Berretas in Don's belt sent them scurrying back to their office, no doubt phoning the cops.

Don ran down the coastal footpath. He was heading for the path that led back to the main road, near the Duck, where he would have a good view of the pub from behind a low wall.

I walked up the road from the Marina and onto the main street. I gave Ronnie a quick call, to tell him that Don had him covered from behind the wall.

Word was spreading throughout the apartments and hotels from the people who had been evacuated from the Duck. They had heard there were armed men in the vicinity. Pools and sunbeds were emptying; people were standing on balconies, nervously looking up and down the main street.

The Moroccans in the cars were growing restless. One man got out of each car and they started to walk slowly to the bar entrance. As they turned the corner from the car park, they spotted me.

I was standing in the middle of the road, about two hundred yards from the Duck. I started to walk towards them, the Russian-made machine pistol in one hand, my stick tapping on the tarmac as I walked towards them. In my ears, Randy Crawford was singing 'You might need somebody'. *You're probably right, Randy.*

One of the Moroccans turned back and summoned the rest of his companions from the car park. I was unmistakable. I was one of the men they were looking for – a cripple, with a black walking stick.

They fanned out across the road. Small arms appeared, 9mm pistols. There were six of them. The only thing on my side was that the machine pistol had the advantage of accuracy over a longer distance. Then other equalizers appeared.

As they walked towards me, Don emerged from pathway behind them, a Beretta in each hand. As they passed the entrance to the Duck, two Mancs, each carrying a 9mm pistol, emerged to join Don.

Behind them, his usual Brooklyn Slugger baseball bat being unavailable, came Yorkie. A visit to the Duck's kitchen had equipped him with a lump hammer and a boning knife.

I caught the eye of the confident-looking Moroccan in the forefront. I pointed behind him. The odds had changed, and not in his favour. His expression changed. It was time for him to fight, fly or surrender. He decided to fight.

I felt the bullet as it caught the sleeve of my coat. It did no damage to me other than a small nick but the shot spun me to my left, causing me to drop the stick. But that freed my hand to control the machine pistol.

I fired a short burst, being careful not to get my allies in the firing line. The Moroccan in front went down; three bullets hitting his chest.

The man ahead of me to the left levelled his gun at me as his head exploded: a perfectly aimed shot from Gary. Manc One had done himself proud.

Don opened fire with both guns, aiming low, taking out legs. I'm not sure who got the other two. Manc Steve and I opened up at the same time, riddling them.

Screams came from the balconies. *Please God, no innocents*, I thought. Four Moroccans lay dead, two crippled, with Yorkie looming over them, looking for signs of fight. There were none.

Then, as we thought it was over, two minibuses appeared further down the street, about a hundred yards beyond the entrance to the Duck. Armed men started to fan out across the street. Ronnie, Bunny and Cabrera ran to join us, picking up pistols from the downed Moroccans. Yorkie also picked up a 9mm.

The Mancs and Yorkie were all ex-territorials and knew firearms basics. Don and I were UK Police trained, but neither

Cabrera, Bunny nor Ronnie had held a pistol before, let alone fired one. We took cover behind the low walls fronting the ground floor apartments, behind parked cars – anywhere that provided cover.

The Moroccans were working their way up the road towards us. This lot had serious firepower. Ronnie ducked as bullets raked the wall he was sheltering behind.

'We only want the cop and the cripple,' someone called out.

'Come an' fucking ger 'em then,' rang out a deep west Yorkshire voice.

'Not as bad as when Millwall came to Elland Road,' a Mancunian shouted to his compatriot, from across the road.

The laughter seemed to incite the Moroccans and the rate of fire increased.

Cabrera had figured out that if you pointed the gun in the right direction and pulled the trigger, you were probably well on your way to success. He crouched behind a Mercedes with Bunny, his back to the approaching killers, turning and rising. He discharged the 9mm repeatedly, eyes closed but pointing in the right direction.

Bunny followed his example and from the other end of the car, the accountant copied the lawyer, putting down a line of fire. The Moroccans ducked, allowing the rest of us to assume a firing position.

Ammunition spent, Cabrera and Bunny ducked back down and as the Moroccans rose, they were met with a fusillade of small arms fire. Two were hit, the Moroccans halted.

We heard the sirens at the same time. The reason we couldn't detect the direction they were coming from was because they were coming from every direction possible. Behind us, from the direction of Amarilla, we saw men in black appearing, heavily armed.

'Keep firing!' shouted Don, wanting to pin the Moroccans as much as possible until the Special Ops men got into position. The Moroccans tried to fall back to their vehicles. Suddenly, both vehicles disappeared in a ball of flame as Uzcudzen, leading the second wave of Special Ops, approached from the opposite end of the street.

Uzcudzen had clearly mastered the art of surrounding things since our adventure in the foothills of Mount Teide when the Russians came to call. From the paths on the seaward side, the Special Ops cops that had arrived by boat emerged onto the scene.

There was no mercy. You don't expect any if you've killed two Spanish cops and a security guard. The courts were not to be concerned with trying these men, only the coroner.

The only survivors were the two in the kitchen and the two with shattered legs downed by Don a few minutes earlier.

I looked around. Cabrera was slumped down, resting on the front tyre of the Mercedes. He gave me a thumbs up, but he looked pale. Ronnie had a few injuries, but he seemed OK. He was being controlled by a Special Forces guy who made him lie down and hand over the 9mm pistol.

Bunny had blood running from his sleeve, but like mine, the injury looked superficial. He was still standing, the gun at his feet awaiting the attention of the Special Ops Troopers.

Steve, Manc Two, was down. He had caught a bullet and lay slumped over. Yorkie was stood dead centre of the scene, lump hammer at the ready but with a look of sheer horror at the carnage.

I couldn't see Don Brown.

Chapter Twenty

Ellen Perez entered Malmo Police HQ. She was met by Detective Commisar Johansen. He was a big, blonde-bearded man, who carried his bulk well; a modern-day Viking if ever there was one.

'Where is she?'

'Under guard, in my office.'

'What is your thinking, Commisaar?'

'Please call me Ingemar – may I call you Ellen?'

They walked slowly across the polished wooden floor of the Atrium that served as the reception area. His blonde Nordic features contrasted with her Latin darkness, made even more pronounced by years of exposure to the Canarian sun.

'She seems reconciled to the fact that she has been conned. She has accepted gifts. I do not believe she realised the value. The information she has divulged is serious. Had she not walked into this building and told us what she did, we would possibly be investigating the deaths of several of our undercover guys, but because of her, we are currently pulling all the undercovers out.'

'At least they're safe now.'

'As of an hour ago, only the guy in Tenerife and a woman in Amsterdam is outstanding and I expect her to walk into a safe space in the next few minutes. So, we have lost information streams, but let's face it, we are going to be fighting this war for decades. Whatever we have lost, we will one day recover, and we haven't lost any agents – so far.'

'What are you proposing to do with her?'

'Before this, she was a good cop. She can never work in the same role again, but I am thinking of using her positively. She is the only person who has seen Kadar, who can positively identify him, who knows how manipulative he is. She also hates him with a passion that you have to see.'

He stopped and turned to Ellen.

'We Swedes are supposed to be cold emotionally, especially when compared to you Latinos. It's not true. Vengeance is represented in our mythology by the god Vidar, whose vengeance knows no boundaries and no end. At his moment, she is a true daughter of Vidar.'

He looked towards the windowed room where Brigit Olsen sat.

'How well do you know her, Ellen?'

'I've only met her a few times, but we got on well.'

Ingemar Johansen looked squarely at Ellen. 'I have a plan.'

Ellen thought back to her sister's kidnapping a few years ago. She had broken every rule to rescue her, exposing herself to dismissal, prosecution, and imprisonment, aided by a ragtag British team of misfits. She'd been saved by a Basque master detective, who believed the Law was an instrument to be used to achieve justice, not just blindly enforced. As a result, she had been redeemed. Her shame turned to determination to do the right thing, not necessarily the legal requirement.

She saw in Johansen a kindred spirit to Uzcudzen. A pragmatist.

'Speak to her, Ellen. If you feel, as I do that by using her skill and knowledge, we may get our hands-on Kadar.'

***

Don Brown was dead, killed by a burst of gunfire from the second wave of attackers with virtually the last shots they fired. Steve, Manc Two, was also dead, lying with his feet in the street and his upper body on the footpath.

Bullet holes riddled the shop fronts, apartments, and bars. Black-clad Special Forces Cops patrolled and searched the area.

Ronnie was being patched up by a paramedic. Wendy came to him and called him a bloody idiot, before throwing her arms around him.

Cabrera too was being tended by his wife. His asthma had kicked in and she was administering his inhaler. People were wandering back into the street.

Bunny stood with Yorkie. This giant, so used to violence, being consoled by a small, studious man, whose first encounter had been intense and deadly and through which he had emerged heroically.

I was standing in the centre of the road. My arm was bleeding through my jacket, but it was only a flesh wound. I was in shock.

A cop came up behind me and took the machine pistol. He emptied it and laid it on the floor.

'Any more I need to know about, Danny?'

'Yes, in my belt.'

He lifted my jacket and took the third Beretta, again removing the magazine and placing the gun down on the Tarmac.

Uzcudzen came up to me, and taking my arm, led me to a chair and sat me down.

'I'm sorry about Don and your English friend – Steve?'

'Are any civilians hurt, Paulino?'

'It doesn't look like it. We are doing house-to-house checks. Everyone seems OK – scared, but OK.'

He made me take off my jacket and looked at the wound.

'Its fine, a scratch,' I said.

I looked down the street. They were placing bodies in bags.

'Please don't let them put Don and Steve in the same ambulance as those bastards, Paulino.'

'I won't, compadre.'

'Jesus, this is my fault.'

'No, Danny, it's just the way things panned out. They would have come here anyway, people would have died anyway – as it happens, you and your crazy gang have probably saved lives.'

Coffee and brandy started to arrive. One of the girls from the Duck brought out a bottle of Johnny Walker Black label, some glasses and a bucket of ice. I downed a couple. It did its job. It usually does, that's what it's for.

I hadn't noticed the music in my ears for a while. But it was unkind of Gregory Porter to be singing 'Hey Laura.' I thought of my wife, Laura, who had dumped me here. If she hadn't, none of this would have happened. I cried.

***

They flew Don Brown's body back to Luton. His arrival was low key, no great ceremony, but a contingent of senior officers as well as old colleagues was there to meet the coffin. He was unmarried. Both his parents took the loss badly, but they had other kids to comfort them.

On the same day that Don was flown back, we buried Steve the Manc. There was a hell of a turnout of expats. The cops provided an escort from the church to the grave. All the regulars from the Duck were waiting at the cemetery. The chief mourners were his business partners, Gary, Bunny and Yorkie, who, in honour of his dead mate, was wearing a specially flown-in 5xl Manchester City top.

After the ceremony, Uzcudzen took me aside.

'We know who authorised the attack on the airport and outside the Tame Duck.'

'Who?'

'It's a Moroccan we've been after for years. He's well connected with the Moroccan government and has bribed and coerced his way into Police and intelligence units throughout Europe. He runs virtually everything that comes in from Columbia into southern Europe.'

'Is there anything I can do?'

'Yes, Danny, there maybe is. What happened here the other day is a major setback for him. His management structure will be badly rattled, his prestige amongst his employees damaged – if we can find a way into bringing him out into the open, we may nail him. Maybe, my friend, your talents as a target could be put to use again.'

Chapter Twenty-One

Kadar sat in the small café and checked the newspaper. He carried a pay as you go phone, avoided any form of social media, and relied on newspapers to keep him up to date.

He had just entered Denmark, the first step along an intended drive of 1500 or so kilometres to Madrid. He knew about the debacle in Tenerife. He was furious about the failure of his men, but he managed to control his anger. His customers and partners would be severely rattled. He started making phone calls, reassuring them that normal service would soon be resumed. He had decided to take the long drive to let things settle, appraise the situation.

The battle of Golf del Sur was well reported. It had made the newspaper headlines, with photos and interviews taken by the apartment dwellers overlooking the scene. The most striking photograph was from early in the incident: eight of his men walking down the road in line. Waiting for them was a man wearing a straw hat and a linen jacket, carrying a machine pistol, leaning on a black walking stick.

He turned the page. In other news, in Malmo, it was reported that a female police officer had committed suicide by jumping to her death from a tenth-floor apartment on the outskirts of the town. Her name had been withheld, but it was understood she worked in the Detective division and was divorced.

Kadar's well-known coolness and self-control was at breaking point. He had wasted time, money and prestige trying to find the infiltrators into his business, and now this bitch had ruined his plan. He would have to go back to the drawing board. At least the price of coke was rising again as the storage facilities in Spain and elsewhere started to distribute stock. The loss of the Tenerife stash was bad, but at least it aided the overstocking situation. Soon he would be re-ordering in vast quantities from the Columbians.

He drove through Denmark until he embarked on the Rodby to Puttgarden ferry to the north of Germany. He drove to the picturesque city of Lubeck, in the shadow of its Gothic cathedral spires, and stayed the night in the Nui Rig, a small laid-back hotel, with low-key, well-equipped rooms. Using the hotel's telephone system, he made several phone calls from his room to his associates and employees.

He turned on the TV. Tenerife was still in the headlines. Senior reporters had been dispatched to the island. Everyone was asking why Muslim fundamentalists (as they assumed) had targeted this sleepy retirement village?

The news report played certain videos which had gone viral, showing how the community had taken on and held a determined team of terrorists at bay. The local Spanish solicitor and his friend, an expatriate British accountant, had emerged from the side of a parked Mercedes and with eyes closed, they had blazed away at the terrorists. A local pub owner, who, they had learned, had never used a gun before in his life, had been wounded, and three British-born diving instructors had also played a key part in the battle; one of whom had died.

Donald Brown, a serving British Police officer, assumed to be on holiday had also died fighting the terrorists. There was another, more mysterious man yet to be identified. He was filmed walking down the centre of the road. He was either handicapped or injured, and clearly needed to use a walking stick, but he had used a very powerful weapon, later identified as a Russian-made machine pistol.

***

Uzcudzen held a press conference, standing alongside the Governor of Tenerife and the Spanish Prime Minister. The Prime Minister was extolling the response of the Police and Special Forces in wiping out the Terrorist cell.

After a series of questions to the politicians, the media turned their attention to Uzcudzen. He was questioned about the community's reaction to the attackers, a few of whom had been identified.

Paulino had planted a question with a press contact. It came towards the end,

'Colonel Uzcudzen, who was the man in the Panama hat? He seemed disabled in some way – he had a walking stick?'

'That man is Mr Danny Maclinden. He is a local businessman, originally from England but now settled in the Golf del Sur. He was slightly injured but is recovering at home.'

***

Kadar looked closely at the image. This was the cripple; the man who had smashed the Venezuelans, now responsible for the deaths of his men. Who was this English bastard? He had to be eliminated.

***

Ellen Lopez entered the small office. Accompanied by Johansen, she sat alongside him, facing Brigit Olsen.

'I can't look at you, Ellen.' Tears ran down Brigit's face. 'I have been so stupid. I thought I was falling in love with this guy – what an idiot I am.'

'You aren't the first, and you will not int be the last.'

'Did they get any of the undercovers?'

'No, luckily we have managed to pull everyone out of the field' said Johansen.

'Don Brown died in a shooting in Tenerife,' said Ellen. 'But it may not be due to you.'

'Jesus, I hope not.'

'Ingrid, we have an opportunity here. You have seen him, Kadar. At last we have someone who can identify him. You can catch him, redeem yourself.'

Ingrid looked up at Johansen with hope in her eyes. 'Anything, absolutely anything.'

'Two hours ago, anticipating your response, I issued a press release regarding the suicide of a Malmo-based female Police Detective. No name as yet. We've planted a body in the spot – it is an unidentified woman we've had on ice for six months. The media has films of the bagged body being recovered from outside your apartment block.'

'So, I am dead?'

'To all intents and purposes, yes you are, it makes you safer.'

'What do I do now?'

'Go with Ellen to Cadiz. Your job will be boring, ploughing through airport arrivals, intelligence pics – anything to get a handle on Kadar.'

Ingrid got to her feet. She hugged Johansen. 'God bless you, Ingemar.'

That night, Ingrid and Ellen waited in Madrid airport before catching the connecting flight to Cadiz. In the airport shops Ingrid purchased enough clothing and essentials to get her through the next few days.

Arriving at Ellen's apartment, they made up a spare bed, ate, showered, and slept. Tomorrow was going to be a busy day.

By eight in the morning, both women were in an office in the Cadiz HQ of the Europol Task Force. They had requested copies of the CCTV images of all arrivals in Southern Spain and the Canaries over the last twenty-four hours.

Quickly eliminating the earlier images, Ingrid focused on the face of every person passing through the immigration checks. It was felt that Kadar, would, as he always had, travel openly and confidently, on an assumed name but with a perfectly legal passport.

The technology was refined to identify people only presenting a Swedish, Moroccan, or Spanish passport, furthering narrowing the field. After two days, when she went back over the images twice, she had failed to identify Kadar. Where the hell was he?

***

The Volvo XC 60 driven by Kadar was a typical, understated quality vehicle, ostensibly being driven by a smart businessman of North African ethnicity. As it crossed the French/Spanish border, it was waved through. There had been no passport checks since the vehicle left Malmo.

Kadar drove to Pamplona. He hadn't seen his associate there for nearly a year, although they spoke on the telephone frequently.

The city was the eastern-most outpost of his empire. Beyond that were areas where the Serbs coexisted with the Bulgars and the locals in the distribution of drugs. Kadar's wholesale operation supplied them all, with entrepots from the Mediterranean coast. Pamplona was, from his perspective, his, with his own distributors, supplied from the Atlantic.

He had his meeting, ate, drank a little, and slept. He was reassured that his associate was comfortable with the situation; that the situation in Tenerife would soon be under control. These things happen, and Kadar was the very man to sort them out. Next morning, he left to drive to Madrid.

***

We had a wake in the Duck. English people don't usually do wakes, but it seemed appropriate, there being a large Irish contingent living in the Golf, many of them good friends of Steve.

The mood was one of sadness and pride, of loss but achievement. The structural damage had been or was being repaired; the shattered windows replaced; the bullet holes plastered over; the blood washed away.

I sat with Uzcudzen and Cabrera as Tommy Loughran, the Irish entertainer, sang tunes of old Ireland, interspersed with the occasional Scottish lament, Welsh songs, and English sea shanties.

'Does he know no Spanish songs?' asked Uzcudzen.

'I doubt it, Paulino. Not many Spaniards come here. Mostly expats and tourists.'

He nodded to Cabrera and they walked together to the stage. As Tommy finished a song, Uzcudzen spoke to him and he mounted the stage, followed by Cabrera.

Standing either side of the microphone, they sang a song I've come to know as 'The Maiden and the Nightingale', a truly beautiful traditional Spanish lament. It was striking that one singer was from the northernmost part of Spain, accompanied by another from Las Canarias.

It reminded us expats of where we were, guests of this great country, of its history, its culture, and the way the Spaniards have welcomed us northern Europeans to its heart.

As they sang, I thought of Don Brown, of Steve, of what we had gone through and how near death we were just a few days before. So did the others. There wasn't a dry eye in the house.

***

Kadar pulled into a service station a few miles before the turn towards Madrid airport. He walked into the café area, bought a coffee, and sat down.

About ten minutes later, two men entered, got themselves a coffee each and joined him.

Aryn was from Uzbekistan, fair hair with blue eyes, an ex-army cage fighter; tough, very tough. Bilal was from Mali, his skin a burnished black. He had spent time with ISIS and other terror groups. These days, he just killed people for money. He was good at it. Neither of them looked like a Moroccan, but they were both loosely connected with Kadar's network.

Kadar explained the situation. Initially, he had intended to kill the cripple and make a show of force against the increasingly intrusive and disruptive police activity. That plan failed, but the cripple was a nuisance. He kept resurfacing; he had to go. The two assassins nodded.

***

An increasingly frustrated Ingrid sat with Ellen as they looked through the images.

'Where is he?' she asked the screen for about the twentieth time.

'Maybe he's sitting it out in Sweden,' Ellen said.

Ingrid sat back in her chair with a flash of inspiration.

'Maybe he's travelling by boat?'

Ellen looked her in the eyes.

'No,' then 'Yes,' she said, as the possibility dawned on her.

They accessed the CCTV records from the obvious embarkation points for someone wanting to use the ferry to Tenerife.

Ingrid scrutinised the arrivals at Cadiz airport. The four pm plane from Madrid which had arrived yesterday afternoon was full, with a long line passing through security. It was an internal flight, so the queue moved quickly.

Suddenly Ingrid stopped the tape and backed it up.

'That's him.'

Ellen stood up and looked over Ingrid's shoulder. Ingrid put her finger on the image of Kadar's forehead.

'That's the bastard.'

Wherever he was, he had a full day's start on them. Their assumption was that he was going to Tenerife to sort the mess out himself. A check of the one possible flight to Tenerife drew a negative; he must be going by ferry. Which meant that when he stepped off the ferry in Santa Cruz, they would be waiting.

There was no sign of him on the Ferry Terminal CCTV, but he could easily be concealed within a vehicle. The earliest he could have boarded a ferry was twenty hours previously, which meant he could not disembark in under forty hours. The journey he was taking, subject to sea conditions, was about sixty hours.

Ellen arranged the flights and she and Ingrid flew to Tenerife, this time to Tenerife Nord, the airport nearest to Santa Cruz.

They were met by two members of Uzcudzen's Praetorian guard, who sped them to the port's CCTV Control Room which had effectively been taken over by the Chief of Detectives of the Guardia Civil and his staff.

There were thirty hours to go before the most likely ferry docked.

They checked into a nearby hotel, they ate, they rested, they slept, they anticipated; they got it wrong.

Chapter Twenty-Two

The Outer Limits SV52 is one of the fastest speedboats in the world. It accommodates four passengers comfortably, including the pilot. It has a half-cabin for the storage of necessary gear.

In this case, it contained three assault rifles, sidearms, six grenades, a supply of ammunition and several cans of diesel. The passengers were the leader of one of the world's leading illegal drug importing cartels and two of the best assassins on the planet.

The boat pulled out of the harbour at Huerta, some miles east of the great port of Cadiz. The experienced pilot, the boat's owner, had already been well-rewarded for his services: a large amount of money had been transferred to his bank account. The balance would be paid later, just the same arrangement he had already enjoyed for many years when delivering contraband on behalf of his mysterious employer. Who, unbeknown to him, was sitting alongside him in the cockpit.

Once out of the harbour mouth, the speedboat slowly picked up speed. Within half an hour, the triple diesel engines warmed to their task and soon, a cruising speed more than eighty miles per hour was achieved.

The boat was heading South, to Tenerife, its snow-capped mountain, its lush, historical north, and the concrete pueblos of the south. And me.

***

Uzcudzen spoke to me every day to keep me updated on any progress. I was permanently armed, now sporting a shoulder holster and an Uzcudzen-supplied and very powerful but handleable Smith and Wesson.

I avoided the Duck and the office, keeping away from crowds, keeping away from everyone. Plain clothes cops had been drafted in from the other islands and from the mainland.

I moved out of the villa and round the coast to Los Gigantes, where massive cliffs dominate the Atlantic and oversee the channel between Tenerife and La Gomera. I found a small apartment for rent, moved in, and waited.

***

The bay of El Medano is usually heavily populated by windsurfers during the day. At night, it is a desolate area, with an occasional camper van or tent, but usually nothing populates the beach.

The SV52 moored about two hundred yards offshore. Three men boarded the inflatable and headed for the beach. As soon as they were clear, the speedboat took off into the night. The three men reached shore, deflated the boat, and stored it in the rear of the waiting Ford Ranger, alongside the bags containing their armaments.

They drove immediately towards the Golf. Reaching the village of Los Abrigos, Kadir stopped the car, pulled out a mobile phone and called a pre-entered number.

'Where is he?'

'Not in the Golf,' replied the spy he had arranged to be inserted into the Golf two days earlier.

'Where then?'

'I followed him to Los Gigantes.'

***

In the Ferry port control room, Ellen and Ingrid surveyed the arrivals. Armed men and women stood by, awaiting their instructions to strike.

There was no sign of Kadar. Armed customs personnel searched cars and lorries; anything that could hide a man. Nothing.

A photograph of Kadar taken from the Madrid CCTV system had been quietly circulated to cops throughout the island.

Uzcudzen decided to tap into the public tension, still high following the Golf del Sur battle. He arranged for the photograph to be released to the media, with a statement from him, giving strict instructions to the public:

'This man is a suspected terrorist. Do not approach, but inform the Police immediately. He is believed to be armed and extremely dangerous'. It made its first appearance on TV at six in the morning.

***

As dawn broke and Kadar and his assassins drove into the town of Los Gigantes, John Macdonald was taking his early morning constitutional, walking up and down the steep streets that caused his heart rate to ascend to the required 132 beats per minute.

He noticed the Ford Ranger first. He liked the make and was considering trading his Isuzu for one. Therefore, he took particular notice of this one.

The driver looked familiar. Had John not seen the early morning news containing the photograph of Kadar, he would have continued up the hill. Instead, he avoided eye contact and took out his mobile phone.

I, too, was out of my apartment. Uzcudzen had forwarded me a photograph of Kadar, some hours before it went into general circulation. I decided to walk along the cliff tops. It was level and the path well-maintained.

My knees could cope with flat surfaces; it was stony and uneven ones that were beyond me. The main reason for the walk was to clear my head and to consider my situation.

I looked over the edge, 2,000 feet straight down. I wasn't considering suicide. Far from it, but if you were going to do it, this was the place. The jump would be painless, but the landing would hurt a bit – although death would be instant.

Billy F Gibbins was singing 'Rollin and Tumblin'. *Yes like that, Billy.*

***

'What do you mean, he's in Los Gigantes?' shouted Uzcudzen down the phone.

'Colonel, a resident saw the TV broadcast at six am. He went out for a jog and the first car he saw was being driven by Kadar. He has men with him. They are in a Ford Ranger pickup – we even have the registration number.'

'Where is he now?'

'Parked in the square – none of the cafes are open yet.'

'How many men have you got in the town?'

'Not enough.'

Two Police Special forces helicopters scrambled, carrying pilots and four passengers. They included Ingrid and Ellen and two teams of Special Forces Troopers. Fast cars were dispatched from all over the island.

***

In the centre of Los Gigantes, Kadar sat and waited. He had not liked the reaction of the old man out walking, but all was quiet. There were no sirens, no blue lights – no one could possibly know he was on the island, let alone this out-of-the-way place. People were waking, some taking exercise.

***

John Mcdonald was, as a resident, a member of the local Facebook group where the expats swapped news and information. After he made the emergency call to the police, he sent a message to all the other Los Gigantes members to tell them to keep out of the square, as the terrorist Kadar, that bloke on this morning's news, was sat there, bold as brass.

As you would expect after receiving such a message asking them to keep their distance, those who had received it went and had a look. Kadar became aware of several old, apparently north European, people, peering over balconies and poking their heads around corners.

He was becoming increasingly twitchy when the cage fighter passed him his iPhone. Kadir looked at his own photograph, plastered all over the local news.

'I thought you said no one knows who you are?'

Kadar, normally so self-possessed, felt panic rising within himself. He started the car and turned it to face the road back to the motorway. As he sped along the road, he saw the helicopters, obviously coming into land.

He saw them just before he spotted the roadblock, Four Guardia Civil cars, two blocking the road and another two pulled up behind them, making any attempts to ram through them difficult, if not impossible. Equally, there were at least six determined-looking cops, all pointing small arms at them.

There was a track to the left. He spun the car towards the track, and climbed, the big 4x4 eating up the gravel as it powered upward. After about a kilometre, the track petered out and Kadar found himself on the cliff top.

***

I turned as I heard a big engine, coming in from the north west – a helicopter, black, no markings, it came in low and fast and hovered just above me. The loudspeaker activated, with a woman's voice.

'Stay where you are, Danny, we're coming for you.'

As I waved to Ellen, the shots rang out. I looked back to ground level as the big Ford raced along the cliff top. From its windows came the obvious sight and sound of automatic fire as its occupants aimed at the chopper.

I looked back up. In the doorway of the helicopter, I saw Ellen Perez slump, as the bullets hit her.

The pilot turned the helicopter away from the line of fire and flew back towards the island's interior.

Dropping my stick, I withdrew the Smith and Wesson. As I looked towards the 4x4, I saw they were focused on the aircraft.

If they had noticed me, they had concluded I wasn't as important as the chopper. Aiming with both hands, my first bullet penetrated the windscreen and I saw a rifle drop from the window. I continued to pump bullets into the interior of the car. The driver lost control and it flipped onto its side.

I started to hobble towards the car wreck as the helicopter, now joined by its partner, came flying back in, the rising sun providing a stunning backdrop.

***

The Ford Ranger had flipped onto its left side. Both Kadar's shooters had been hit and incapacitated by the shots from the handgun.

Kadar had been injured by the impact of the car turning over. Blood dripped from his forehead. He managed to open the door and climb onto the side of the vehicle. He reached for his pistol. Looking up, he saw a lone figure with his back to the cliffs. Kadar raised his gun.

I shot him in the hand. Kadar screamed and fell from the car. I walked over to him, writhing in pain, the blood flowing from his ruined hand.

'You -?' he said, gritting his teeth in pain.

'Me?'

'Who are you?'

'Just a cripple from England, by way of Golf del Sur.'

'You're a nobody.' His lip curled and he spat at my feet.

'Too good for you though, eh, Kadar,' I said.

The helicopters landed. A blonde woman in combat fatigues ran towards me, gun in hand, leading her team. I put my hands up, just in case.

'Are you Danny?' She was Scandinavian, good looking,

'Yes Ma'am, at your service. Is Ellen OK?'

'She is hit, Danny. They are working on her.'

Kadar looked up at this blonde apparition, realisation sinking in just before she kicked him in the balls.

He was on his knees now, with his back to the cliff edge. As the information about Ellen sunk in, I lowered my arms, then raised the gun, pointing to Kadar's head.

Kadar heard the click. As the hammer hit the empty chamber, he reached for the pistol in his ankle holster, smiling. My gun clicked again. Ingrid turned to me.

'Stop, Danny.'

I continued to limp towards him. Kadar brought up the small pistol and struggled into a standing position. I threw down the empty Beretta.

I heard a familiar voice call me. It was Ellen.

'Danny – here.' I half turned as she threw me my stick. I caught it and in one move, threw it at Kadar.

He was about two meters away from infinity. He staggered as the stick hit him hard. He stepped backwards and joined my faithful African hardwood stick as it started the fall to its watery resting place and Kadar's oblivion.

I stood on the cliff edge with Ingrid and Ellen and we watched the final moments of Kadar and the stick. I knew I would miss the stick.

In my ears, Billy Joel sang 'Only the Good Die Young,' *Wrong, Billy.*

Epilogue

The fish of the day was Cherne, or Wreckfish, often misnamed as Sea Bass. It was served with Canarian potatoes, salad and a nice Lanzarotean white wine.

    I ate alone. Nearby, Bunny and Yorkie were playing cards with Cabrera and Gary. They had all been away for most of the day, probably a fishing or diving charter. Wendy was in the kitchen and Ronnie and the barmaids was running the always busy bar.

    Uzcudzen had phoned to give me an update on Ellen. She was badly bruised, but the Kevlar body armour had done its job.

    The press had been placated with a story about the terrorist Kadar committing suicide by jumping from the cliffs at Los Gigantes. His companions had been taken to the intensive care unit at Santa Cruz but had died of wounds sustained in a gun battle with the Guardia Civil. I was surprised at this news, but they were both wounded and it's a bumpy road from Gigantes to the ICU.

    I settled back in my chair and moved the metal, clinic-supplied walking stick that had replaced my African hardwood. I sipped the last of the wine as the card game ended and the Arsenal versus Chelsea game started on the big screen TV.

The Duck would be male-dominated now for two hours whilst the game was on. Then it would give way to the night, the ladies, and the music. Tonight, there were quite a few ladies in early. There are worse places to be than the Tame Duck.

The door opened and in walked two of Uzcudzen's apprentices. They took up positions at either side of the entrance, leaving the door open. In walked Paulino, flanked by Ellen and the Swedish lady cop, Ingrid.

I started to rise as they approached my table but Uzcudzen gestured for me to remain seated.

Ellen took the metal walking stick and sneered at it. She looked sore, but OK. *Oh, that hair.* She smiled at me. I wasn't good at smiling but I did my best.

The TV had been turned off. The locals and the tourists and the bar staff were looking over towards me. The kitchen emptied. I was clearly the centre of attention.

Uzcudzen spoke. 'Ladies and gentlemen, Senors and Senoritas, many of you who joined in our fight against terrorism and evil – who I may now call colleagues and comrades. I am here to inform you of the result of an enquiry regarding the loss of vital equipment during out latest battle against the Terrorista and the criminal Kadar.'

The faces of those listening were serious.

'As part of our investigation some days ago, the Guardia Civil hired the services of our friends here.'

He indicated the table where Yorkie, Bunny, Gary and Carbrera were seated.

'They carried out a search of the waters off Los Gigantes, and they have been successful in recovering a vital piece of equipment essential in our fight against international criminal activity.'

He beckoned Ingrid forward. She was carrying a long box.

'I ask *mi buena amiga* Danny Mclinden to show you this invaluable weapon,' Uzcudzen said.

Ingrid passed me the box and, somewhat bemused, I opened it. There, in all its glory, oiled, with a gold-coloured ferule and gold inlay on its handle, was my African hardwood stick. Along its length, in small golden letters, was written *'Justicia'*.

Printed in Great Britain
by Amazon